Ambrose Conway

THE RESO
A Sixties Childhood

KINGS HART BOOKS

First published in 2007 by
Kings Hart Books
An imprint of Publishers UK Ltd
26 Beaumont Street
Oxford, England OX1 2NP
www.kingshartbooks.co.uk

Second edition published 2009

Cover design: Luke Hughes and Ben Overton © 2007

ISBN: 978-1-906154-01-1

A CIP catalogue record for this book is available
from the British Library.

To
Graham, Crid and Jack at the time,
and Jane, Luke, Owen, Georgie and Bazzie
with whom anything is possible.

About the Author

It is said that if you can remember the Sixties you weren't there. Ambrose Conway was there and has almost total recall of his formative years.

Ambrose is a former secondary school teacher and educational consultant who has a particular passion for developing positive reading habits among teenage boys who are so often lost to fiction. He has taught in rural, suburban and inner-city schools and has successfully tested out many of the ideas for The Reso on his unsuspecting students.

He grew up in the old Welsh storytelling tradition and recalls the ancient tales of the Mabinogi read in school as well as the stories of hardship, poverty and joy recounted by his parents.

Access to educational opportunity has been a decisive influence in his life and the inspiration for this book and its forthcoming sequel, Beyond the Reso.

Ambrose Conway is a regular contributor to the educational press with articles on e-learning, raising achievement and inclusive learning among his credits. He has spoken at regional, national and international conferences on similar themes.

Married, with two children, the contrast between his children's upbringing and his own prompted the writing of The Reso as he found himself constantly comparing the quality of his own experiences of childhood with that of his own sons.

He divides his time between schools, military and industrial archaeology, flying, keeping on top of the garden, reminiscing about the past and worrying about the future.

For interactive educational resources on The Reso please visit
www.the-reso.co.uk

Wonderboy, life's just begun.

The Kinks

THE RESO
A Sixties Childhood

CONTENTS

Introduction

So this is what really happens...
Primary school – all the time in the world to muck about, play in sandpits, annoy people and try and stay up late.

Secondary school – starts with such great intentions and excitement – that first page of the new exercise book – the determination to do well – followed by the first mistake and the descent into... Whatever!

Each year then seems to move faster than the one before and you find yourself wishing your time away with – "When I'm in Y9 things will be great. When I'm in Y11 things will be brilliant."

There is a desperate need to be older, to be able to *do* more, and you find, to your surprise, that things don't get remarkably better, they just change: primary school turns out to have been the golden time and all the adults are banging on about, "the best years of your life" and it doesn't seem like that to you.

But you know that when you are in your twenties it really will be great. No one telling you what to do then. Party time! But your twenties come, and you find yourself working and with responsibilities and people demanding your signature on countless paper documents.

So maybe your parents are right? As if!

And so it came to pass one dark November evening that I was late coming home from work. The street lights were already on and had turned from that vivid orange to that dull, boring headache yellow.

I was tired and the air was damp. I parked the car carefully in the garage and shoe-horned myself out of the driver door between the boys' bikes and numerous cartons of paperwork.

It had been a bad day. I pulled the garage door down and some water that had been idly gathering there for a joke cascaded down on my trousers, causing me to drop a work file. Rude words came out, not so loudly that the neighbours heard but loud enough for me to feel better. I reached for my door key and dropped another file of work on the damp door-mat.

The family were cocooned inside, warm and content. From the kitchen to my right came the smell of spaghetti bolognese. From the living room to my left came the strangled nasal whine of the latest two-day wonder band that the boys were watching, transfixed.

It came from deep back in my throat. It needed no thinking about and it could not be stopped, it just gushed out.

"My God! You call that singing – you can't understand a word they're saying! Any chance of a tune breaking out or is this it? What do they look like!"

I didn't get any further. My wife burst in to reveal the amazing truth – I'd turned into my father. For this was a repeat of an outburst he had shared with me some twenty five years before.

So be warned – you do turn into your parents.

I thought I'd better tell you about the shape of things to come before I forget.

Chapter One
THE RESO

I didn't realise until someone unkindly pointed it out to me, but the large council estate on which I was brought up was known as 'The Reservation'. To those who lived in the posher areas of town, the drives and crescents and boulevards, we were considered, "the savages from the reservation".

The name stuck and slowly we learned to take delight in our notoriety. We became the Reso and our savage behaviour, or rather our reputation, was feared throughout the town. Not that the Reso was a particularly fierce place, except at certain times. But, then again, I never knew anything different so it seemed natural to me.

The Reso was a vast council estate carved out of former marshland which backed on to the river. It resembled a huge Dairylea cheese slice cut out of the western side of the town. The railway formed the northern boundary and a dilapidated industrial estate made up of corrugated iron buildings painted in that strange green flaky paint, which looks old as soon as it is applied, completed our quarantine. We seemed safely cut off from the civilised world.

The practice in those days after the war was to build on a massive scale, hundreds of houses on one site. The houses quickly filled with soldiers returning from the war and their young families, which tended to expand at an alarming rate in what became known as 'the baby boom'.

The houses were substantial and of good quality. Everyone had three bedrooms, one of which was so small it was habitually known as the box room, not that we ever had sufficient boxes to fill it.

Downstairs, a living room and an equally sized dining room were laid out. Most of my friends lived in the room designated 'the dining room' as it lay between the kitchen and the boiler hidden in the fireplace. It was by far the warmest room in the house and, in those pre-central heating days, this was a major consideration.

Despite the pressure on space, I do not know one family who did not use the front room as 'The Best Room'. This meant that it was decked out in the best materials, wood panel linoleum, Remploy furniture and an expensive looking three-piece suite bought on the never-never (except in our house where my mum and dad did not hold with tick).

The walls held family pictures telling the world, or whoever was invited in, who we were and where we had come from. This was echoed on the sideboard where a picture of the family on our one and only foreign holiday dominated. The only other pictures were of my brother and me in our school uniforms, me with my school captain's badge on.

I always felt that if the worst came to the worst, and the police called at our door, these pictures would be used as a silent reference to our character. For that was the point of the front room. It was not for us, it was for visitors and guests, a place to show, a place to talk seriously on special occasions.

The garden was an undoubted asset to the house. The passion of the time was to plant privet hedges to soften the menace of the ring wire fence which marked off all the borders. The square front garden had a substantial breeze block wall some two feet tall and the gateposts were made of a two foot square pillar of bricks capped with crenulations to resemble some castle gatehouse.

Our gate was always open, which rather spoilt the defensive effect. The wall was the scene of medieval carnage though, as we played 'bestest falls', which meant that we pretended to walk along the wall, oblivious to the hidden archer in the privet who would pretend to shoot us. We, in turn, would pretend to be shot and fall spectacularly from the wall to the grass below. Whoever made the most spectacular death dive got to be the archer and the process was repeated until we got bored or someone fractured a wrist in an attempt to outdo the others.

In the dry soil that abutted the house, my dad had planted some bulbs that appeared like fireworks every summer.

There was a front porch fringed by a semi circle of bricks and, unlike most of the houses on the estate, which were bare brick, ours was coated in flaky whitewash. I was always intrigued that in the mortar of the wall that supported our full length back gate were some airgun pellets. I wished I had an airgun and I dreamt of the marksman who had many years before left his mark in the drying mortar. Apart from the marksman, I was the only other person who knew about the pellets and it was a secret I enjoyed.

The tall gate meant that the alleyway at the side of the house was always dark, damp and windy. It always gave me a bad feeling, unlike the moss which congregated around the large iron manhole cover that we used to step on to hear its metallic thud. At the end of the alley, to the left, was the kitchen door, painted corporation light blue. Ahead was the space for the bin and behind that the substantial shed and outhouses. There was a toilet which we only used in emergencies, a coal hole which was replenished with a hundredweight of coal every week in the winter, and the shed itself which doubled as an aircraft cockpit, the wheelhouse of an ocean liner and a convenient place to mope when in trouble.

Behind the shed, under the rusted metal-framed windows, was a dumping ground for garden waste and an old bike, and from here I could climb onto the fence post and then lever myself up onto the thick, concrete shed roof. This was a fair vantage point because, as ours was a corner plot, I could see the gardens of a fair selection of my best friends. On Bonfire Night, as dusk fell, I always ended up here, from where I could observe the first of the rockets erupting, and smell the tang of freshly lit fires.

In the winter of 1963 the snow fell so deeply and the wind blew so strongly that a magical drift appeared which reached up the eight feet to the top of our shed and I longed to have the courage to step off the shed roof into the inviting snow and ice.

My dad had masterminded the design of the back garden. He could be very deceptive in such enterprises. Without fuss, he could turn his hand to most things and I was surprised to come home from school one day to find the garden, which had previously been rough ground over which my mother would only venture in her garden boots to put out the washing, staked out with string and wooden markers to a grand design of some magnitude.

From the shed to the end of the garden near the rabbit hutch, the outline of a path appeared. This continued along the fence at the end of our plot. Wooden battens had been used to delineate the path and my dad was busy breaking up council paving stones to use as hard core foundation. It was one of the best times to help him and be deemed useful on such a major engineering project.

To smash things in a constructive manner and mix the sand, cement and chippings so purposefully was incredibly fulfilling. When we finished, we both stood back, as workmen do, and surveyed our work. We declared ourselves satisfied with our labour. I was proud to be included in the "How do you think we've done?", and was sorry when the project was finally over.

The downside of this building work was that the mud pathway along which I had taught myself to ride a bicycle by holding on to the clothes line with one hand whilst steering the bike with the other, was obliterated. No bad thing really, as I had managed to pull half a washing line down on one effort. That had been a very bad day.

The substantial rabbit hutch, another of my dad's projects, housed Snowie and a series of ill-fated companions. Amongst them were Blackie the intrepid black rabbit who attempted to head butt his way through the chicken wire, and Stripey the grey and black rabbit, who exploded with diarrhoea. On reflection, we were not particularly original in our rabbit naming.

Snowie, though, did seem a permanent fixture in my formative years, predictably nibbling on some vegetable matter and producing copious amounts of small black excrement, which I once convinced my young and hungry neighbour were actually currants.

This was the safe bit of my life, and I knew every inch of it. Outside our house you moved with some caution. There was a lot to think about as you moved about the estate: who to offend and who not to, when to gamble and when to keep quiet.

Mums on the estate were usually pretty accommodating, unless they went out to work, in which case they were invariably very harassed. My mum did not hold with mothers going out to work whilst little ones were of school age and said so on a regular basis until she too went off to work when we hit a period of cash embarrassment.

Dads were a different matter. Most of the dads on the estate worked shift work in the factories down the coast. The pattern of changing shifts from mornings, days and nights completely destroyed their sleep pattern and left them tired and irritable. The downside for us was that no matter what hour of the day we chose to play around the houses, there were a number of dads trying to snatch a few hours sleep at the same time. This was bad chemistry. Never more so than when the dad in case of point was Sammy Barker.

Sammy was a wiry man with highly serviceable trousers held up by a thick leather belt, black army style working boots, an iron-singed shirt, a florid face and thick metal rimmed glasses. He had a large number of children, estimates vary, but collectively they were known as the Barkers in the same way you might refer to a disease as scurvy or rickets – a nasty bout of the Barkers. Even by the low standards of our estate they were notoriously combative and easy to provoke. In the normal scheme of things you would wish to avoid them, but Sammy was fatally attractive to me.

The reason for this being that he was frequently full of ale and, on his circuitous journey home, when he drifted down our avenue, stopping only to engage in an animated conversation with the pillar box, alternatively agreeing with the pillar box and then falling out violently with it and cursing its parents and its redness, he would focus on me.

In many respects what followed had much in common with cobra baiting. I tried to sway backwards and forwards in time to Sammy's meanderings. "All right Mr Barker?" I'd venture as politely as possible.

"All right lads!" he'd reply, which was strange when there was only me there. If I was lucky he would go on to a kind hearted ramble along the lines of …

"You're a good lad you are. I like you lad, you're always very polite. I know your Dad I do. Here son, get yourself and all your mates some sweets."

At which point the contents of his pockets would be proffered. Invariably this would include sweet wrappers, betting slips and the inevitable dirty linen hankie but also assorted loose change and occasionally a ten shilling note.

He'd shamble on and I'd pick the assembly of money from the floor and treat myself to some chewy sweets and the latest ice lolly sensation. However, such occasions were outnumbered at least four to one by a different interchange when Sammy would turn ballistic at any mention of his name.

"I know you - you cheeky little sod. Come here and I'll take my belt to all of you!"

At which point I'd leg it and Sammy would be left talking to the post-box, "I know his Dad, you know. I do." And the post box would stand in silent agreement.

The thing was, you never knew which Sammy you were going to get from one occasion to the next, and he would not remember you from one meeting to the next, which made it both potentially dangerous and potentially profitable – but apparently he did know everyone's dad.

Chapter Two
GRAND NATIONAL

You may think from reading the above that I was a cruel and vicious exploiter of Sammy Barker and his fondness for drink. You may think that my efforts took food from the mouths of his clamouring and numberless brood. In one way you would be right, but in another, so, so wrong.

You see, there was a history to this relationship – and a history from which I still bear the scars, literally, on the backs of my legs.

The sporting year on the estate mirrored national sporting events for us youngsters. Football was played all year round naturally, on roads, paths and on the recreation ground, with its three pitches with sagging and paint chipped metal goalposts.

Cricket was played for a very short window of a couple of weeks in the summer until we all got bored because Ronnie would have an innings as the West Indies and would be in for four days – whacking the ball all over the park as I attempted to imitate the full England side, bowling and fielding. Eventually he would declare on several thousand for four wickets and would proceed to skittle me out for about seventeen if I was lucky. Mind you, I was only up for this kind of humiliation a couple of times in any one summer.

The Grand National had greater significance then than now, when it competes with legions of television channels showing every conceivable sporting occasion. We would celebrate the Grand National in the park by replicating fences from freshly mown grass, including the infamous Canal Turn, Beechers and the Water Jump. I remember it as the only time I wore my school cap – to replicate my favourite mount, Arkle, or rather his jockey. We'd race twice round the perimeter of the playing field with as many as forty lads joining in, falling and jostling each other until Ronnie inevitably won.

Given the monotony of winning, it was Ronnie who came up with the Grand National variation – we'd jump the hedges and ornaments of the gardens in the avenue. Number sixteen's pond feature would be the Water Jump and Sammy Barker's five foot tall privet hedge would double for The Chair. On paper it seemed a great idea. The only problem was we were not going to do it on paper – we were doing it on foot and that could only lead to trouble.

The occasion of the first running of the Grand National proved a great success, as did the second. Twelve and sixteen starters respectively all crouched behind the concrete wall at 2 Gwynfryn Avenue ready for the off.

And then away like bats out of Hell.

Ironically, the first hedge we jumped was my own. But with my dad at work and the front room unoccupied, as no state occasions were taking place, I felt relatively confident that we would not be detected. I even tut-tutted with my Dad when he inspected the damaged hedge later, and vowed to aid him in bringing the miscreants to justice. Even so, I felt a pang of guilt as I crashed through three feet of privet at the point that I knew it was thinnest. My pang of guilt was undoubtedly less severe than Martin's pang of pain when he attempted the hedge at its thickest point and was upended, his feet describing a very neat circle in the sky as he went.

Not all parents were working, and not all front rooms were unoccupied however. The secret was to keep up with the front runners. This meant that by the time a parent had spotted you, registered that someone was ploughing through their hedge, reached their front door and hurled abuse "I know your bloody father!" - you would be a distant blur beyond a large acreage of privet whereas the tail-enders would risk interception.

The only issue here was that they might grass you up, but being Reso kids they knew better than that!

"I was sitting minding my business when I was coerced by some boys THAT I HAD NEVER SEEN BEFORE to jump through some hedges. The boys were NOT FROM ROUND HERE. I think, judging from their accents, that THEY CAME FROM SCOTLAND OR INDIA OR CHINA OR VENEZUELA. I would not recognise them if I saw them again."

That's how their statements would undoubtedly have read.

You can have too much of a good thing, however, and the third running of the Grand National was a race too far. Conditions seemed perfect, dry underfoot and a slight breeze at our backs. The third running had the added fear factor of the possibility that the adults would be wise to the event. A certain amount of adrenalin kicked in when you knew parents were ready to give chase to you – it was the physical equivalent of turbo-charging. Tired legs suddenly found new fuel and arms flapped faster to drive you forward, a string of abuse bubbling towards you from frothing parents left in your wake.

I always had the desire to laugh hysterically at such times, which was a bad thing as it invariably brought on a stitch which stopped me running in my tracks.

By the time we hit number ten's hedge, parents were appearing at the door of number six – no worries for us, but it meant the imminent demise of Kenny, whose asthma and general flat-footedness had always made the Grand National something of a risky enterprise. But then every street has a plucky Kenny, always game, always caught.

The next fence was the Water Jump because there was an ornamental bird bath which the first to the fence would habitually knock over, scattering the last of the thirsty birds in a major flappage. No fallers at this one, although Kenny, red faced, was trailing and panting heavily, parents in lukewarm pursuit.

The widow lived in the next house and in deference to her we avoided her hedge and ran through the little gap between the hedge and her front window. We were trying to be helpful and sensitive but this was probably lost on the widow who would have seen a herd of speeding spectres smudge past her window closely followed by a stream of parental invective.

Sammy Barker's was next and I naturally veered away from his house to the outside of the track so that I could leap out of the race and away if he was lying in wait for us. To my surprise and alarm as I glanced towards his house I caught a vision of him in the front room picture window.

He stood like a portrait in his belted trousers and casual attire of string vest, glasses askew and enigmatic smile, like a council house Mona Lisa. I naturally accelerated to hit his hedge on top and roll off into the next garden. To my surprise, Sammy made no move, his enigmatic smile following my path to the end.

The impact on top of the hedge instantly revealed the enigma. A series of equidistant stabs of pain punctured my back and legs and I tumbled from the hedge in a gashed and bleeding heap, all forward momentum gone.

Sammy had laced the hedge with barbed wire – he had even painted it green to disguise it. The green paint wasn't even dry as it now flecked my t-shirt and trousers and mingled with the rosettes of blood appearing through the gashes in my clothing.

A joke is a joke but this had gone too far and my first thought was to go straight home and tell my mum on Sammy Barker. The hopelessness of the situation then dawned on me.

"I was sitting minding my own business when some Hungarian boys that I had never seen before made me jump through hedges..." It would never work.

Neither could the truth save me from damnation.

In the end I went to the local cut and jumped in, rolled about in it and went home claiming that some big lads, whom I had never seen before, and who looked foreign and spoke with strange accents had pushed me in. I had cut my clothes on the terrible things that people had thrown in the stream and I was worried about catching that disease from rat pee that my mum was always warning me about.

It was a bit over-elaborate but the talk of rat pee was enough for my mum's protective instincts to kick in. The mud from the stream disguised the paint and I was sent for a bath and bed with a biscuit and some milk. The incriminating clothes were quickly disposed of in an effort to prevent an epidemic of rat pee disease infecting the estate. Job done...but some unfinished business with Sammy Barker to take care of. Hence the drunken Sammy baiting outlined in the previous chapter.

Chapter Three
FAIR

There was a pattern to the year that was very reassuring – as I suppose it is for every youngster. I always felt particularly lucky to have my birthday in October as this conveniently divided the year up into thirds bounded by Christmas, Easter and my birthday.

I always felt sorry for anyone whose birthday fell around Christmas and who would suffer the fate of relatives lumping together birthday and Christmas presents into a single present to serve for both. They would also miss out on the individual fuss that a real birthday demanded, lost in the hullabaloo that was Christmas.

I had lost one birthday, confined to bed with mumps unable even to sit up, and hearing a procession of relatives and friends arriving downstairs laughing and joking on my day, and unable or unwilling even to present themselves in my bedroom.

I was left there sipping Lucozade, which I only had when I was ill and which always therefore brought back unpleasant memories of illness. Only Auntie Dorothy had ventured upstairs to see me and left me the customary large bar of Cadbury's Dairy Milk. I came close to choking on this as I tried to guzzle it in one sitting to make up for the washout of the day.

I'd always felt sorry for Jesus, it was bad enough to have one's birthday on December 25th, but the unpleasantness of Easter must have completely ruined the year for Him.

I'd also lost one Boxing Day when all the family came to our house for revels. This was a self inflicted loss as I had become greedy. I thought I could squeeze in a ride in my uncle's car (a rare treat) with being back in time for joining in the fun with my cousins. Unfortunately, we had gone to pick up my uncle who was a vicar in Wrexham, and the slow journey in foggy conditions, coupled to meeting and being entertained by my uncle's spinster landladies who proffered copious amounts of mince pies, led to my delaying the homeward journey by being sick in the car. We arrived home in time to see the last of my cousins disappearing down the road. I was gutted – a highlight of the year ruined.

Christmases always had a predictably cheery pattern. Third week in December, trim up and decorate tree – to do so earlier would have been vulgar. With luck, my dad would be on a night shift so that we could share the balloon blowing. Invariably we'd all be laughing when racing to blow up the balloons and would have one blow back on us, filling our mouth and lungs with high pressure air and making a disgusting grunting sound emanate involuntarily from our noses. We would make our own trimmings each year from cheap crepe paper in garish colours. There was an art to intertwining the different colour papers which my dad had mastered. This was one of those surprise discoveries you make about your parents – that they have talents from past lives of which you know little. In this case, my dad had worked straight from school in a grocer's and had learnt such decorative arts as well as parcel-making at which he was a smooth master.

A number of wall-mounted decorations were carefully removed from the cardboard storage box and placed in their traditional places on the wall. These decorations, comprising balls and bells which concertinaed out in coloured paper, were past their best but no one had the heart to throw them away.

The tree lights would be brought out and my dad would wrestle with them as if they were an illuminated boa constrictor. He would always insist on checking them before they went onto the tree. They would never work and he would invariably have to check all the fittings before finding the errant bulb and replacing it. This he would do, commending himself on the foresight to have bought an additional bulb the previous year. He would then drape the lights around the tree trying to distribute them evenly. Finally satisfied, he would step back and ceremoniously switch them on – only for them to remain lifeless and lightless. There would be much cursing before another loose connection was found and eliminated. We would then dress the tree with a mixture of old and new decorations.

Again, many of the baubles had seen better days but were such a traditional part of the festivities that they could not be disposed of. One gold and silver bell predated my birth and I always treated it with particular reverence.

I played the 'If' game with it - the game I played on the pavement walking home from school. If I can get to the next telegraph post, walking normally, before the next car overtakes me then something good would happen, like chips and egg and beans for tea. And then I would walk manically if I heard a car approach to make sure of this treat for tea. If I was responsible for breaking this bell I knew terrible things would follow. So I always carefully placed it at the heart of the tree so that it could not be knocked in passing and, even if it did fall, would simply nestle in the branches. It was, thankfully, unlikely that it would be dislodged as I secured it every year with two paper clips and some sellotape just to be on the safe side, and took it off and placed it in an egg carton on each sixth day of January.

Luckily, nobody ever noticed my bizarre behaviour in the frenzy and I was never asked to account for this strange ritual. The child psychologists would have had a field day. Generally I was disorderly, but here were 'obsessional' and 'compulsive' making an early appearance.

We decamped to the front room for Christmas which gave it an extra edge. Knowing that we were living in the special room heightened the appeal. It also meant that when the presents had been distributed I could stretch out on the carpet and play to my heart's content with my latest goodies, model soldiers or tanks, a train set or Scalextric.

The train set was one of the best presents. It amused me for hours, recreating scenes from my train-spotting on a small circle of track. There was also the added advantage that if I set out the track near the cat's traditional sitting spot, she would invariably play with the train as it came round towards her. As she settled down with her tail across the track I'd suddenly turn up the voltage on the transformer and she'd shoot out of the room like a scalded... well, like the proverbial cat. I'm sure it did not hurt her as we would repeat this experience day after day. Looking back, this either meant that this did not hurt her, as I suspected, or alternatively, perhaps she just had a short memory which is not something I had considered at the time.

Late Christmas Day we would all make for my Nain's for a gathering of the clan. There were never less than twenty of us for Christmas Tea. The table to accommodate us stretched from one end of the room to the other and comprised every table in the house, interlocked. Once you were sat down there was no further movement allowed.

On top of the electricity cupboard was an artificial tree and I obviously followed my Nain in hoarding Christmas decorations, as she had some small decorative crackers with photographs of grotesque clowns on them. These predated the war and always gave me the creeps. I thought the clowns must all be dead or well beyond their clowning prime by now and every year the sight of them made me sad.

In the table placing lottery I once drew the short straw and wound up with my back to the roaring fire. My nain had a way of building a fire, learnt in service in a big house as a girl. She would stack the coal so that it took up all the space in the grate and spread right up to the chimney. Suffice to say that had my nain been a stoker on the Titanic it would have been moving so fast as to have scythed though the iceberg – melting it as it went. In the unlucky year in question, I could feel the lacquer on the chair melting and, although the heat was intense and made me feel sick, I would not forego the marvellous treats on display on the table.

My mum and aunties, once we were settled, would bring us an unending array of goodies. Many of these were only seen and tasted at Christmas. There was cold turkey, beef and ham, potted pastes, shrimps for my uncles and thickly buttered bread. My nain used Lurpak butter which always tasted luxurious and I always associated its taste with high living. For each of the children there was a special Hovis loaf, a large un-sliced loaf in miniature.

Adorning the table were some highly seasonal treats which we did not see from one year's end to the next. Pickled onions vied with red cabbage, beetroot and bits of cauliflower and other vegetables in vinegar of which the most offensive were gherkins. One of my cousins had once told me they were pickled slugs and I can never get that image out of my mind. There was fiery mustard and unusual cheesy biscuits in sticks and balls, all within arm's reach.

I think it was at this meal that I developed the habit of constructing sandwiches with such precision. Beef with mustard on the Hovis roll followed by turkey on white bread with pickled onion, repeating until I could eat no more.

The soundtrack to this meal was provided by my uncle, who, somewhat surprisingly, given his usual persona, and no doubt fuelled by drink, would delve in his record collection and provide the habitual record for the meal: One Thousand Welsh Voices singing arias from the Albert Hall, and The Vienna Boys' Choir seasonal message or lessons and carols from Kings College, Cambridge. It boomed out over the meal adding to the mood of excess - heat, food and sound.

Jelly, trifle, mince pies and Christmas pudding was the unvarying sweet selection and, despite feeling fit to burst, I was not going to pass up on this second phase. By now the parents had retired to the kitchen to pick at the turkey carcass and open the bumper beer can, laughing and joking, and reviewing the year and previous Christmases which always seemed even better than this one. This allowed us cousins to renew old rivalries and do disgusting things with the food.

By an act of will, when the meal was cleared away and we were sunk in settees, chairs or sprawled on the floor, we would manage the odd After Eight mint or Matchmaker as we drifted off to sleep, with full stomachs, in the hot, airless atmosphere. This, I felt, was how it was meant to be and I always hated it when the mood was broken by the late night walk home, even though it was made special by seeing the coloured lights displayed on the white ice cream dome of the Pavilion Theatre, which then towered over the other buildings on the West End of the town.

Boxing Day was a repeat of these rituals at my house, and, with me on home territory, I had the deciding vote on what games my cousins and I would play. Life really did not get much better.

Easters in general scared me. Good Friday probably scared me most. First, because we would have to get dressed up and go to church when it was not even Sunday. Second, because we always had to have fish and parsley sauce for dinner and fish scared me. Third, because I was always worried that at three o'clock the world might end because it always went really dark in the epic biblical films when Christ was crucified, and there was a particular hint of menace about them. All that hymn singing about green hills without city walls and how wicked we all were always made me gloomy, and old people dominated the congregation like ghosts.

The Good Friday service always rotated around the churches and when it was in Holy Trinity, the oldest church in the Parish, I always freaked. The other churches were light and airy or large and imposing, but Holy Trinity was squat and oppressive, with wooden seats worn by excessive use to an unnaturally dark colour. The rose window above the altar did inject some colour into the building, but only managed to highlight the dust and decay in the air.

Once, the sunlight bursting through the window was obscured by clouds and the light suddenly dimmed. I was convinced the end of the world had come and that I would die there horribly, wearing shorts, knee length socks and a tie with an elasticated loop round the neck. Even if I was miraculously spared this fate, I had haddock and parsley sauce awaiting me. The Apocalypse seemed preferable.

The other reason I hated Good Friday was that it set the tone for a miserable weekend waiting for the action to begin on Easter Monday.

Easter Saturday was just another Saturday with more visitors to the town than normal. This meant that the family would have all the more reason not to venture out as the roads would be full of coaches and caravans. It always seemed to be sunny and windy on Easter Saturday and we always ended up flying kites which was OK. Easter Sunday started promisingly with the doling out of Easter Eggs but we were not allowed to eat them until the evening, so that was another day wasted. Songs of Praise and that Sing Something Simple, where harmonious people would murder songs from the old days, really put a crimp in Easter Sunday. It was all too much, hanging around for Monday.

But Monday, when it came, was always worth the wait. For on Easter Monday, come hell or high water, my nain would insist that the whole family, all thirty of us, go for the afternoon to the Marine Lake and Ocean Beach Fun Fairs.

Being a seaside resort, Rhyl had two permanent fun fairs which were open from May to September. They would always open on Easter Monday to test the rides – "With human guinea pigs," my dad would always say. We were allowed two shillings each (10p*) and this would secure eight rides at 3d each or a combination of rides and slot machines.

One ride was obligatory – the miniature steam train around the lake – a mile and a half journey during which the engine either condensed steam in oily droplets over your face or deposited black sooty smuts on your clothes. The track meandered through the rides before heading out around the lake in which people boated or drove speedboats sedately around a fenced track. The ten-minute journey

_____

* A shilling was the equivalent of 5 new pence, but it was 12 old pence.

gave you time to savour the impending excitement and make a final decision on which rides to patronise – the old favourites or the new attractions.

Most of my cousins would scurry from the train to the roller coaster whilst I would feign more interest in the dodgems. The truth was that the rickety old wooden coaster petrified me. One year the little voice in my head became somewhat distracted in the hullabaloo and I ended up pushed into the queue and onto the ride. My cousins – some of them girls and younger than me - were genuinely excited as the ride climbed up the chain fed incline, but I was frozen with fear. The slope felt endless, and the whole creaking structure seemed to sway in the light breeze. On the way up, although my muscles seemed so tight as to prevent me actually turning my head, my eyes could flicker from side to side and note the incredible gradients of the dives and whooshes ahead of me.

Whilst they screamed in delight as we endlessly accelerated and gyrated, lockjaw prevented me from even changing facial expression, and the little voice in my head panted, "Almost finished, almost finished, just one more dip, then almost finished," in a strangulated little echo which I never wanted to hear again. I could hardly release my grip as the ride clattered to a halt and I had a horrible feeling that something tremendously unwelcome had happened in my trousers on the way round. This was doubly worrying as, in fact, I was wearing shorts. I quickly concocted a story, "Did anyone else have manure thrown at them on that ride? There'll be trouble if I catch who did it. Look at my shorts – ruined! I'll not be going on that ride again."

It was implausible even by my standards, and luckily the scenario was avoided by the discovery that cousin Jane had dropped her candy floss over my legs in her excitement. I never did ride the coaster again.

I was a demon on the dodgems though. The secret was to take it personally and stalk your prey patiently, catching them on the flank as they were about to turn, so that their car almost toppled over. I'd mount a series of such raids against those most unlikely to retaliate. But there were good and bad cars and these changed each year as they were maintained, so you might end up, with adrenalin running, in a car that moved like an invalid carriage, whilst enduring a battering from your jubilant cousins. I'd always make a mental note of which cars were lively and would forfeit a ride rather than end up in the crip.

The carousel spooked me – the horses' faces had the look of things that nightmares were made of – the mad, staring eyes and abundance of teeth always made me shudder. In later years I did not like Tony Blair for the same reason.

I could manage the waltzers, no matter how fast they were spun by the ne'er do well who operated the ride and fiddled the change. It was less than magical how he could palm you sixpence change from the 3d ride when you had given him a shilling. Invariably, if an auntie had paid for a group of us she would be short changed and he would feign no knowledge of money he had taken seconds before. If the case was pressed to the ride controller then the spiv would suddenly remember the correct change, but in truth, fiddling the punters was the accepted practice of all who made a living from the fair. Coming from the Reso, we had no problem with that as a general principle but thought it a bit off that they should try it on with us rather than the foreign holiday-makers.

Over a number of years, I built up courage to go on the Satellite, a number of rocket shaped cars suspended from arms that spun round at seemingly amazing speed. The beauty of these cars was that there was a joystick in each one which fed compressed air into a ram which enabled you to control the height of the rocket car. Mine would be the one that would flit about just four feet off the ground whilst my cousins' cars were spinning thirty feet off the ground with the cars inclined so that they were leaning out almost horizontally. I'd complain when the ride ended that my rocket had a malfunction which prevented it rising skyward, but I was rumbled when I tried this excuse three years running. Vertigo had struck me once again.

I'd be happy in the Caterpillar, which was a swift, undulating roundabout over which a canvas descended, but the Rotor, a huge centrifuge in which the floor fell away leaving you pinned to the wall, and the Octopus, which was like the waltzers in three dimensions, were beyond me.

The climax of the visit, at the far end of the Ocean Beach, where the sea air mixed with the fried onions and toffee apples, was the Mad Mouse. This was a huge metal edifice of a ride on which four-seater, mouse-like vehicles lunged around, steel wheels screeching on steel tracks, making sharp, insistent ninety degree turns at great heights, punctuated by witless dives through the metal superstructure. I would always pretend to be deliberating on which rides I wanted to revisit at this time, whilst my mum would unhelpfully suggest I went on the Mad Mouse with everyone else. Habitually, I would end up forfeiting money at the end of the day because I had avoided going on so many rides that scared me witless. I only hoped, year after year, that none of my cousins would rumble me.

The Easter Monday treat would always end with chips from newspaper on the way home, and a visit to Sidoli's Italian Ice Cream parlour. This was as exotic as Rhyl could manage, a genuine Italian family serving genuine cappuccino coffee, although we called it frothy coffee then, from a machine that sounded like a consumptive clearing his throat.

Outside Sidoli's was a massive ice cream cone some three feet high and made of plaster. I always imagined being served one that size inside. Unfortunately, Sidoli's imagination, or our budget, only ran to a standard cone with a Cadbury's flake.

When the adults had finished their chin-wagging it was back to our house for the first salad of the year, and we would all play in our back garden, come rain or snow or shine. I thought it would always be like this, but I suppose that simply showed a lack of imagination.

Chapter Four
BONNY

The American tradition of Halloween had made no purchase on our imagination as youngsters. In school we were told that Halloween was the night when the fabric between the real and the after-life was at its thinnest and that all manner of spirits roamed the earth at the witching hour of midnight.

Frankly, this gave me the willies and I was mightily relieved to know that I would be carefully tucked up in bed, facing away from the window and with the curtains and my eyes firmly closed at midnight.

There was no trick or treat and our attempts to scare each other in the dark were essentially no different from any other dark night of the year. Nobody came a-calling and if they did, demanding money with menaces, they would be given short shrift by all our parents. For some, demanding money with menaces was such a regular theme of their lives on the Reso that it seemed pointless to try and confine it to a single night.

One year, Halloween was characterised by a howling wind that set the trees dancing and clouds scudding across the moon. I was really unnerved by it and retreated indoors to watch Z Cars and drink sweet tea by the family hearth rather than brave such elemental forces.

On a braver Halloween night we did try to summon the dead with a giant Kalamakulia to which we all contributed a firework. James, who must have been feeling particularly flush after a visit from his auntie from Nottingham, weighed in with a one shilling Roman candle, whereas the rest of us could not muster more than a tupenny banger, although Ginger Rodney managed one of the enticing red Little Demon thrupenny bangers.

We argued for fifteen minutes about the merits of foregoing the resonating explosion of the Little Demon in the confines of the entry between our houses for the contribution the little red peril would make to the gunpowder stash for the Kalamakulia.

In the end, we decided that the Demon would be ignited in the entry following the Kalamkulia and that everyone had to stand no more than three feet away from it when it exploded so that we all shared in the delight, and cemented our friendship through defying fear. We knew from the last time we did this that we would spend the next half hour sharing the experience of our ears ringing and all attempts at talking reduced to even more high-pitched gibberish.

Six of us danced round the pile of assembled gunpowder which had been carefully stripped from the fireworks. Unbeknown to the rest of us, James had inserted some indoor firework snakes into the mixture. We had a false alarm when little Robbie ventured out onto the pavement to join the revels and we had to convince him that we had no fireworks, that we were not behaving suspiciously, and that we were not trying to usher him back indoors as quickly as possible.

We had to be silken in our cajoling. There was no use in threatening him as he would simply go indoors and report to his parents that we had fireworks, and we would be chased off to inconvenience some other family down the street. All the time we were convincing Robbie to disappear, the gunpowder risked getting damp or a sudden gust of wind distributing it harmlessly across the estate, and that would never do. He stumped around passing our gunpowder pile twice, almost walking through it the second time. Finally, boredom at watching us studiously doing nothing over an extended period led him back indoors and we returned to the revels.

Six times we danced clockwise around the assembled pyre of gunpowder and six times anti-clockwise chanting "Kalamakulia, Kalamakulia!" and barely able to contain our laughter in the excitement. We looked like the atavistic natives in the King Kong film, trying to placate the great Kong with the sacrifice of the waif-like Fay Wray. Our sacrifice was no less sacred – over three bob's worth of pocket money. Finally, as one, we stopped and James struck the match, holding it aloft briefly to catch before slowly arcing it down to the thin, three foot trail of black powder which formed a fuse leading to the main pile of mixed gunpowder.

The gravity of the occasion was, however, lost when the match of our High Priest went out in the wind. Muttering "Bugger" he lit another, and without ceremony, threw it on the pile of gunpowder that formed the fuse.

Never before could such a pile of gunpowder have been assembled to placate the god, Kalamakulia. Three shillings worth of the stuff! We trembled at the prospect that such a pile of gunpowder could unhinge our world in its sheer magnitude.

The fuse caught and we watched saucer-eyed and wide-mouthed as the white smoke set off at a brisk pace to the mother-lode. A small mushroom cloud of smoke plumed, followed by a faint crack of white, red and green light as the disembodied Roman candle followed its chemical script. We craned forward, disappointed at the minimal impact of our ritual and accumulated three shillings of gunpowder.

At this moment, the residual heat of the small but intense conflagration ignited the firework snakes, which unwound at alarming speed and shot in unpredictable directions straight at the assembled worshippers. We turned and fled at this unexpected turn of events; even James who had planted the snakes in the first place. The six of us departed the epicentre of our worship like a shock wave of banshees, screaming and hollering. Within seconds we had collapsed on the pavement in laughter and gathered around the nearest lamppost to relive the tale and prepare the scale of exaggeration ready to re-tell to friends in school the next day.

It was half an hour before we were ready to share the delights of the Little Demon in the entry. It did not disappoint and we were once again forced to leg it with our ears whining like the television once the programmes had finished, and James dad's clenched fist remonstrations sounding no more than a furious bee in a distant, sealed jam jar.

On reflection, that was the best Halloween. But Halloween could never be more than the countdown to Bonfire Night.

Bonfire Night was a premier night of the year.

Before the advent of the vast communal firework displays, and the regimentation of the health and safety brigade, Bonfire Night was as significant a family occasion as Christmas. Any family with children had their own fire and fireworks in the back garden, with neighbours invited.

My family was no exception, and again, our house was the location for the annual gathering.

Before the rough ground was filled in by my dad's rose garden and lawn, we assembled a fire in the very centre of our garden. The spot where runner beans, carrots, onions and strawberries grew in the summer was cleared and left fallow for the fire. Packaging and any surplus wood were consigned to a holding area out of sight behind the shed.

I'd inspect it daily, turning it over to make sure it remained dry, and scavenging any spare plastic sheeting to shelter it from the rain. In truth, the bonfire pile was better looked after than Snowy the rabbit. I'd watch the omens carried in the weather in the run up to the night, and hope that the heavens would empty themselves of rain in the week before the fifth, and be too exhausted to dampen our night.

School would do its best to wind up our sensibilities on the day of the event. Mr Roberts, the Headmaster, would always read graphic accounts of the capture, torture and trial of one Guido Fawkes, and would sign off with an afterthought that Parliament and Democracy were important parts of our constitution which always needed to be defended.

We'd be lost in pictures of Guido on the rack, limbs popping and blood oozing. Ginger Rodney reckoned he could have coped with the pain of the rack. So James gave him a Chinese burn by way of a test and he whelped loud enough to disturb the assembly. Everyone looked in our direction, including the assembled teachers on the stage.

Simply by following the direction of the turned faces in the Hall to its epicentre it was immediately clear that Ginger Rodney was the source of the disruption. Although the craned heads of the pupils had transgressed the unwritten law, that you never grass anyone up, they had simply looked instinctively and *en masse*. I was particularly impressed with James, who was now looking at Rodney incredulously, as if to state, "I can't believe that you interrupted what our esteemed Headmaster was just saying about the importance of democracy as the foundation of this country!"

Nice one James. For myself, I'd have happily carried a placard that read "It was him!" with fingers pointing down on Ginger Rodney's head. I'd have sung, "It was Rodney Williams who shouted," in Gregorian chant if it had added to the discomfort of my regular tormentor.

"Rodney Williams! Outside my room now!" and without a word Rodney skulked out, red face contrasting nicely with his freckles, like a currant bun on the rise in the oven.

He would be forced to stand on the spot of shame, an indentation in the parquet flooring in the corridor which had been worn down by generations of miscreants awaiting their fate in the Headmaster's office, and anxiously dissembling or assembling excuses.

He would be standing opposite the painting of the old Welsh woman in a decorated shawl in some rural chapel. It was said that if you looked closely in the decorated shawl you could see the face of the devil glaring back at you. I hoped Rodney was being suitably tormented now. He would be forced to stand next to the framed exhortation that Manners Makyth Man – which could almost form his charge sheet. I'd always been surprised that the school had allowed such a glaring spelling error to be displayed, but mine was not to reason why.

Best of all, everyone in assembly would slowly parade past him in his shame on their way back to classrooms. This prospect would be so delicious that I conspired either to circle the quadrangle of corridors twice or be sent on an errand for the teacher so as to drink deep in his discomfort. I knew of old that Mr Roberts liked to savour his humiliations and interrogations.

I'd once been falsely accused by a teacher of climbing on the school fence to get a view of my parents coming up the road for sports day. It was to have been, due to shift patterns, the only time my dad would be able to attend my sports day, and I was spurred on to look through the hedge, but I never climbed on the railings.

The teacher in question, clearly on a short fuse with all the last minute sports day preparations, showed uncharacteristic venom in sending me to stand outside the Head's office. An hour slowly passed, with my having contributed mightily to the indentation in the flooring, driven by the prospect of my parents attending the sports day only for me to be unavailable due to detention. Luckily, Mr Roberts came out of his office, and asked what I was doing malingering around there when I needed to be out with my form for Sports Day. Whether it had been an omission on his part, or a reflection of my previous good character, no more was said of the incident, and I was mightily relieved.

There would be no such acquittal for Rodney. He was a serial offender.

The afternoon of Bonfire Night was always characterised by painting, and we eagerly set up our easels and newspaper in Miss Settle's class and attempted to capture in the thick paint, that we had to make up from copious tins of powder, the spectacle of the night.

Miss Settle, a palpably good person with the patience of a saint, would try to encourage us with the inspiring pictures of the Masters, using light and shade. I remember a flurry of blue that was a Van Gogh, it seemed clear to me that he had attended either the most expensive firework party in history, or had been very drunk at the time of executing his painting.

There was a picture by a man called Mondrian, who had reduced his painting to a number of coloured squares. I could not see a bonfire in it. I thought that was just lazy and lacked skill, and shared the thought with Miss Settle, who, to my surprise, was anxious to hear more art criticism from me.

She always listened intently over her ornate glasses and under her immaculately assembled hair. She always, in one way or another, asked you why you thought that and waited patiently as you attempted to form an answer. Sometimes she waited a whole two minutes, which seemed a lifetime but once getting you talking, she seemed genuinely keen to listen to your ideas. I'd have liked Miss Settle as an auntie, not only because she was such interesting company, but because she would also buy you the best presents, craft kits and puzzles which were 'educational'.

My painting had started well with a clear ground established in brown and a sky in black.

"Paint what you see in your mind's eye," exhorted Miss Settle.

I glanced over at the easels of a gaggle of girls who seemed to be effortlessly applying paint in subtle daubs to craft a scene, whilst engaging in earnest conversation about something other than Bonfire Night. My two stripes of brown and black seemed inadequate somehow. Perhaps I was the Mondrian of the class and would be subject to the same dismissal on completion of my painting.

I blew on my sugar paper canvas, keen to get the undercoat dry so that I could apply the detail. The more I blew the more the colours ran and the undissolved grains of powder paint stood proud of the paper, creating ugly irregular blotches. In disgust, I tried to smudge them out with my finger, which merely blurred the distinction between brown and black. Night ran headlong into the ground. I decided to move on by choosing a smaller, clean brush to punctuate the sky with stars in the hope of conjuring up a clear night. The white paint ran into the black before I could form the distinctive shape of childlike stars. I mixed some dark blue to try to reform my stars more distinctly but this too bled into the surrounding colours and made the sky ominously cloudy.

Exasperated, I moved on to add exploding rockets, Catherine wheels and Roman candles, with the same result. I was now staring at a canvas that was a uniform dark purple in colour. My artistic attempts had been reduced to a single coat of horrendous dark puce emulsion. At that moment Miss Settle appeared at my shoulder and remarked, "An interesting treatment of the subject, David…" She stepped back to consider and continued, "Does Bonfire Night have some particularly sad memories for you?"

I failed to put my name on my work and left it to dry on the big table, keen to spend the last minutes of what had been an interminable afternoon listening in the quiet corner to Miss Settle reading from the Enid Blyton book, and scanning the sky regularly for any ominous clouds. As the bell sounded the end of the day, for Miss Settle's benefit, I folded my painting carefully and carried it out of the room and into a waiting litter bin.

The most enticing piece of advertising ever dreamed up by man was the artwork on the cover of the family pack of Standard fireworks (10 shillings and sixpence). It was an explosion of jagged colours in vivid blues, reds and yellows, set against a darker blue field. It was everything my artwork wasn't. In October, it was featured in television advertising and although our television was black and white, I always saw this advert in colour and sang along to the theme "Light up the Sky with Standard Fireworks". I sang it to remind my parents that they needed to set aside funds for the purchase.

I never knew which of my parents purchased the box, I assumed it was my father, as it was really Man's work. Whoever it was, I never found the box before the night when it would remarkably appear and all the fireworks would be decanted into a metal biscuit tin. They knew that had I found it, the temptation to reach within and snaffle through the yellow tissue paper for favourites to share with my gang in the nights leading up to the fifth would be too much.

Held loosely within the box were large traffic light fireworks which erupted in reds, yellow and greens. Volcanic cones all called Vesuvius which crackled and spilled out silver magma with an insistent crackle would glower in the corner. There would be the obligatory bangers with blue fuses and black and white chequered bodies of cardboard wrapped tightly to enhance the explosion. A further rummage would produce that most demonic of fireworks, the jumping jack, a coiled spring of gunpowder folded on itself to contain a series of unpredictable bangs hiding in each fold in the gunpowder. Whether by accident or design, these always seemed programmed to follow unerringly the path of any excitable females in the bonfire congregation, and they would be pursued around the garden, each bang bringing forth a female scream. This was such a wilful firecracker.

A further rummage would produce an aeroplane, a firework with a cardboard wing attached, which would rotate and leave the ground at impossible angles. Sadly, both the aeroplane and the Jacky Jumper were to be banned on safety grounds by the end of the decade, much to our disappointment.

A Jacky Jumper had once lodged in the new suede boot of my Auntie Mina and had exploded three times without her being able to unzip the boot and remove it. It had caused serious damage to her lower leg and no doubt such regular accidents repeated across the nation contributed to its demise.

The firework box would contain some make weights, small Roman candles which would either produce a spectacular result out of all proportion to their size, or sparkle with such promise only to fizzle out in a second.

We were heartily encouraged not, in any circumstances, to approach the latter, but in my head I could hear the firework god Kalamakulia imploring me mentally to note where the failed fireworks lay on the ground, and to gather them up for the following night's gunpowder communion.

Our box of fireworks was supplemented by those of all the attendees, and I was keen to encourage as many visitors as possible to contribute combustibles. I even sought out peripheral friends of our family who I knew had no siblings and indifferent parents who would be happy to donate to our party. The year I invited lonely Howard, I was amazed to see him arrive with a three foot Deluxe box of Standard's, which had cost no less than three pounds. He was my best friend for the night as we gleefully turned his parents' contribution to ashes.

Uncle Roger was something of a connoisseur of fireworks, and not for him was the pre-packed box. He once took us firework shopping in Fell's Arcade, in the town, and we were able to make our own selection from the vast, enticing selection held inches away behind glass. I missed the final selection as I had to go outside because I was hyperventilating with excitement. But I knew I could trust Uncle Roger to mix a range of rockets with plastic nose cones which rattled with promising explosives, and a range of large display fireworks with complicated fuses which linked the various elements. They were called Banshee Howl, The Vampire, Meteor and Satellite, Golden Buddha and Silver Streak, and conjured up precise onomatopoeic pictures which never disappointed on the night.

Given that we would have, on a good night, upwards of two hundred fireworks, we could stretch out the revels for over three hours. Each firework on average would take a minute to select, set up in the earth and ignite, watch, ooh and aah, and review.

This meant that, given the young age of some of my cousins, the bonfire would be lit no earlier, and no later than 6.30 p.m. It was an interminable wait between my arrival home from school at 3.45 and the appointed hour. I checked and rechecked my equipment, my wellies were dragged from the shed, my fawn home-made balaclava was thrust into the pocket of my black gabardine raincoat, and my gloves retrieved from the deepest recesses of the airing cupboard.

By 4.30 dusk would be upon us and I'd venture into the cold garden and climb up the support of the chain fence onto the roof of the shed to sit motionless, watching for the first of the fireworks. In truth, the only fireworks erupting at this stage were those let off by my fellow miscreants or those from families with very small children who would be safely abed before the main ceremonies started.

With the vigilance of an astronomer awaiting a meteorite storm I'd scan the horizon for silver or gold arcs punctuated by distant explosions of colour. I waited with the same anticipation as when trainspotting. The frequent disappointments of a cheap rocket seen only from the corner of the eye were punctuated by the rare flashes of a spectacular symphony of fiery dahlias in full view.

My bum would be numb on the concrete roof when the first of the cousins would arrive and relieve me of my lone vigil. Alan, Kath and Gary would rush out to find me, whilst their parents would add to the accumulated firework and food mountains. Tim and Jane would follow soon after. Young Chris, Steven and Suzanne were only allowed out briefly before the fireworks began and thereafter had to be content confined to the living room with their mums. Their appearance at the window would be marked by the drawing of the curtain along the metal curtain track. They were unhappy at being on the spectator side of the spectacular, and their faces were both slightly sullen at being held behind glass, as well as excited as they stood on the window ledge with their mums supporting them and chattering constantly.

The older children would now dash indoors to implore the adults to begin the fire, but nothing would start until the six o'clock news finished. By design, the news would always include a homily on the dangers of fireworks, and interviews with firemen and casualty staff who were 'braced' to react to the flurry of calls the night always brought.

We knew we would not move the adults before the news had finished, so returned to the kitchen to examine the food that was in various states of preparation.

My mum dished out the first of the tomato soup from a massive saucepan that I can only ever remember being in daily use for steaming the most stubborn stains off handkerchiefs and 'smalls'. On reflection, I'm hoping this last memory is a false one. With polystyrene cups to warm our hands in increments we went out to inspect the bonfire and make sure it had not got damp in our absence.

In the excitement, one of our number would always dash back indoors with their muddy wellies on and would incur the collective wrath of the adults as they trailed mud from the red quarry tiles of the kitchen, over the wooden-floor linoleum of the hall and into the green carpet of the back room.

Having finished the soup, and with cream of tomato lipstick and running noses we would congregate at the kitchen door for food or fireworks.

The hot dogs would not yet be ready as they were meant for the climax of the night. My mum would caramelise onions in the frying pan and cook copious amounts of Espley's sausages in the sweet oil. These would be transferred in batches to keep warm in the oven and would be served at regular intervals with what my mum delicately referred to as finger rolls.

Auntie Dorothy would supply Bostik toffee, so sweet, glutinous and syrupy as to induce confectioner's lockjaw, although, on the metal tray on which it was served in the cold garden it was hard and brittle. Within seconds of chewing it melted and moulded itself to the roof of the mouth in some sugary parody of a dental plate. You were left slowly asphyxiating as it slipped to the top of your throat and dripped into your gullet, sending your breathing into spasm. But, if these had been my last gasps of breath on this earth – what a beautiful way to go.

A large tin of Cadbury's Roses would be available in the front room without a supervising adult carefully rationing the volume and choices of sweet we made. I could easily have sated my appetite on a continuous stream of orange or strawberry flavoured chocolates, but this was the one night of the year when chocolate held no appeal for me, and I made nothing more than a quick raiding venture to the sweet tin to secret a dozen sweets in my bedroom before returning to the garden and the fiery revels.

The Guy would always be placed in the outside loo for safe keeping. During and after the war my parents had mentioned that the face of the Guy was made up to look like Adolf Hitler or Tojo, the Japanese leader. As my family were socialist to the core our guy always had the face of the Conservative Prime Minister and I remember Macmillan, Douglas Home and Heath all succumbing to the flames, and the satisfaction it gave all of us.

When all was ready we would be given a sparkler each and allowed into the kitchen to light it on the gas stove. There were so many of us that our collective attempts to make an aerial ballet of our lighted sparklers was always thwarted by the first going out before the last could be lit. These were dangerous times as the excitement was so overwhelming that sparklers were waved and flourished without any regard to one's neighbours. The worst injuries we sustained were the result of trying to hold on to the bitter end of the sparkler with gloved hands. Several cousins bumped into me and managed to singe my gabardine raincoat, which I thought was a good thing as it would mean I could wear my blue anorak to school, but the following morning my mum declared the damage superficial and, to my disappointment, announced that there was still, "years of wear" in the coat.

My dad was now advancing purposefully to the bonfire, Guy Heath under his arm and matches ready. Uncle Jim, always one to inflame the situation, poured a small container of petrol on the fire, "Just in case". He never explained just in case of what, but it appealed to all the children. He also omitted to tell my dad what he had done. My unaware dad lit the bonfire to an unexpected 'WOOF!', and he leapt backward as fast as I had ever seen my dad do anything.

We were off and running, literally, with a bang.

The start of the display was always heralded by some of the cheap rockets. Launched from jam jars they sizzled skywards and petered out disappointingly, and I looked with satisfaction towards the shed where the spectacular rockets were stored for the climax of the display.

For three hours as many as twenty children and adults were transfixed by the riotous colour and noise, punctuated only by the occasional dud which halted proceedings. I mentally noted the location of all these fireworks so that I could reclaim the gunpowder as I had promised myself earlier. In the window, the youngest of the children were now asleep in their respective mothers' arms but we continued beyond our bedtime, energised and fizzing like the sparklers we held.

Finally, it was the turn of the big rockets and the five did not disappoint with giant red, green and blue chrysanthemums etched against the cloudless sky and innumerable silver explosions erupting staccato style from single rockets. This had been the best firework display to date and would set a very high standard for the following year.

By now much of the fire was reduced to embers with the occasional flames, and, with the adults having withdrawn indoors, we cousins dared each other to firewalk in our Wellingtons. Bravado and stupidity combined and I braved it longest in the fire with the soles of my Wellingtons now melting into a rubbery sludge and the acrid smelly of burnt rubber replacing the heady smell of the fireworks.

We had put potatoes in silver foil in these embers, as we did every year. As every year, our potatoes were baked, trampled, blackened, contaminated with molten rubber and generally ruined now. And, as always, we were forced to fall back on the potatoes my mother had put in the oven as a precaution against this annual eventuality. These were served with a filling of beans and melted cheese and, having been out in the cold so long, we all burnt our lips as they came into contact with the hot tatties. Not that we cared.

Chapter Five
ROBBERY

Where I came from on the Reso, it was assumed that at some time or another I would indulge in a little pilfering – it was only to be expected.

But it was not to be. I have always thought that anyone who embarks on a criminal activity, be it small or ambitious, lacks a certain imagination.

What must go through the criminal mind? Not a lot, I always thought.

Either the criminal did not think he, or she, would get caught, or they did not think at all about the consequences of their action – to themselves or their victims.

So, on the warm and restful summer's day, when I stood outside Barton's shop and contemplated my first formal criminal act, the chances of my pulling it off were not very good.

I was about to steal some sweets because I had never done it and all my friends had. I was about to steal some sweets so that I could tell my friends that I had stolen them and experience, first hand, the thrill of the criminal. I did not want the sweets. I had already resolved to throw them away or give them, with a studied coolness, to my friends – casually mentioning that I had nicked them.

The sweets were not what this was about – it was the experience of the illegal act .

Many of my friends had not had to arm-wrestle their conscience to get their petty criminal careers launched. In some cases, I knew, such criminal activity was a major part of the family income. The rules for this more professional approach were very simple. You did not steal from your own, which was why the actual crime rate on the Reso was so low. Except when one family came into dispute with another. At this point it really was gloves off time as the contents of each other's houses were steadily pilfered. The net effect of this senseless activity was the contents of the combatant's home were slowly moved from one house to the other – a different type of changing rooms.

Generally speaking, the target for youngsters' shoplifting efforts tended to be big rather than small enterprises. The move from those old-fashioned shops where everything was behind glass, behind the counter, and the shop assistant brought you the goods, to the new self-service emporiums, provided ample opportunities.

Woolworths was a favourite target as it had a large, and largely unsupervised, pick-and-mix counter, with tonnes of goodies to hand.

The more accomplished of my shoplifting friends approached the task with a certain audacity. Like some pilfering bullfighter, they teased their quarry before going in for the swipe. Martin was probably the most accomplished lifter. I never did reckon out why. Perhaps it was his dexterity, perhaps his bottle or maybe the fact that his parents were away from the house for so much of the time that he did not fear the consequence of a police knock on the door, as there was a better than even chance that there would be no one there to answer it. Eventually, the police would simply give up and move on to other things. I knew I would not have that luxury. That was the nub of the problem. I saw such pilfering in a very different light.

The vision of me as a shoplifter went in slow motion like this…

Me in Woolworths looking furtive and conspicuous.

Me carefully pocketing selection of penny chews and liquorice laces.

Me moving stiff legged and too fast towards the door, carrying large sign stating APPRENTICE SHOPLIFTER (*What will his mother say?*).

Me outside shop, pockets fully of booty, feeling triumphant.

Instantaneous thud of heavy hand of shop detective on my shoulder.

Me confined in scowling manager's office waiting for police to arrive.

Me interrogated roughly by police in small, dark and smelly cell.

Me taken home to confront my parents. Parents' faces looking like family of the face in the picture 'The Scream' to the accompaniment of my mum howling, "Noooooooooooooo!"

Me confined to bedroom for rest of natural life.

And that, in summary, was why I never shoplifted. No matter how I tried to edit this film in my head, it always played the same and always in black and white.

Martin's film was obviously very different and, no doubt, in glorious Technicolour.

Martin enters shop, helps himself to handfuls of sweets and walks away scot-free to enjoy his ill-gotten gains on the beach. How I envied him at times.

And yet, despite all of this, the urge to be part of this group and to wear the badge that nicking from Woolworths conferred remained strong. Especially as there was now a whispering campaign against me, when Kenny, of all people, mentioned the fact that I was always conspicuously absent from the Woolworths expeditions, with some lame excuse.

My first thought was to batter Kenny to a pulp for exposing me so cruelly, but I quickly rejected this, not on humanitarian grounds, I'm ashamed to say, but merely because the others would have come to the conclusion that there must be something in Kenny's claim for me to react so violently, and then I'd never hear the end of it.

I made a mental note to visit grievous harm on Kenny at some later date, when the link between his accusation and my revenge had been severed. He'd mistime a tackle in football or drop a sweet on the floor, and I'd set upon him in a terrible, mauling flurry. There was something to be said for this, as being utterly unpredictable was the mark of the hard man.

"Don't mess with him," they'd say, "he's totally unpredictable! He hospitalised Kenny for dropping a sweet last week."

And I'd wallow in the notoriety.

I knew this worked as Caroli, the hard man, had visited such a fate on me the previous week. Caroli was a lad not to be messed with. He had the physique of a full grown heavyweight boxer in the frame of a twelve year old. He had what we considered a quirky personality on the Reso, although the professional opinion of a psychologist would probably run to a thousand pages before concluding 'homicidal psychopath!' in capital letters.

A few nights before, I had been coming home from town when I spotted Caroli, on the same side of the road as me – too late as it turned out. There were no roads leading off between me and Caroli and no visible reason for me to cross the road, as the far side of the road was merely the spiked metal fence of the railway sidings. There seemed little incentive to add to my grave situation by giving Caroli a potential weapon on which to impale me. As with bulls, running merely incited Caroli, and he was a better runner than I was. So I was forced to bluff it.

I continued on my intercept course, desperately wondering what I could say in a friendly and casual manner. The problem was that, even in my head, everything sounded several octaves too high.

We drew almost level and I managed, "All right Steve?" in a high pitched trill which had dogs for miles around suddenly alert. There was no reply and I thought I'd pulled it off when there was a sudden explosion of air and I found myself bent backwards over a brick wall. Caroli had one hand on my throat and one held aloft ready to deliver the inevitable blow.

"Were you staring at me?" he asked menacingly.

The killer question. The options were few. "Yes" would instantly bring the nose spreader into action. "No" would prolong the agony for the supplementary question, "So, you were ignoring me then?"

Same result.

I bowed to the inevitable and said nothing, probably because his left hand had by now squeezed my Adam's apple into my mouth and had removed any powers of speech.

After a five second eternity he pulled me off the wall, rearranged the collar of my shirt and said, "Good lad. I hate squealers."

I tried to smile, conscious of the pattern of rough brickwork which had been imprinted across my back. And that was that, Caroli was receding into the distance and I looked the victim of my own personal tornado. That was what I would visit on Kenny in an unsuspecting moment.

Nevertheless, I decided to do some shoplifting research of my own.

I chose my target carefully. I could have chosen Auntie Darly's for an easy target. Aunty Darly's was the school tuck shop. A musty old shop, poorly lit and with penny chews invitingly close to pocket height. But that would have been wrong. Aunty Darly knew my mother. Aunty Darly had served my mother when she had been a school child. Aunty Darly was kind and fair. It would not have been right to steal from Aunty Darly.

Once I had seen one of my friends try to steal sweets from the shop and he had made such a ham-fisted effort of it that even Aunty Darly had noticed the Mojos and Fruit Salads disappearing.

"Well boy," she had said in a matter of fact way, "if you are that hungry you had better have them without paying for them, here have a drink of orange as well."

And she carefully poured a penny's worth of Corona orange into the dainty glass and handed it over. The boy was too stunned to move and merely held out his hand, accepted the glass with his best, "Thank you," and turned a shamefaced red. In that act of kindness she had shamed the lad totally and I vowed never to be put in that situation. No, it wouldn't be, it couldn't be, Aunty Darly's.

I chose Barton's because there was always an air of indifference in the shop. The middle aged, unkempt woman who took over the shop from Mr Barton in the mid-afternoon was always deep in conversation with the other women who came in to the shop for the odd groceries. She was content to let you rummage in the boxes of sweets and then hold up your grubby, sugary hands for a quick reckoning. She had short-changed me many times before and this gave me further reason to target the shop.

Besides, because she left the reckoning to the end it gave the maximum opportunity to pocket the sweets – up to the last moment I could plead that I could pay for them and deny with hurt surprise the suggestion that I was about to steal them.

It all went to plan. The sweets were in hand, and the hand was sidling down to my side and hovering over my pocket when a thousand voices exploded in my head. The loudest voice was my mother's telling me how proud she was that I had never brought the police to her door, unlike most of my friends. That was the clincher and even before the plump shop assistant could glance my way with an accusing stare. my hands were raised, proffering two palms full of liquorice and chews and jelly dummies.

She bagged them and once again over charged me. I turned on my heel moved off from the shop and was brought to a stand fifty yards away when self disgust got the better of me. I can't remember whether I was more disgusted by the fact that I was prepared to steal the sweets or the fact that I had been too scared to go through with it.

Either way, the moment of madness had passed and the remembrance of it meant that I was never again even remotely tempted to steal things from shops. That, of course, was always likely to get me into trouble with the more criminally inclined of my mates who stole because they liked the excitement, and they also liked the taste of the sweets obtained by the five-fingered discount.

Chapter Six
TEA

B ut I had stolen. It was in the family, though, so it didn't count, did it? My criminal undoing, and the reason that my mother's voice was the loudest in that orchestra of angels, was an incident two years before which we had vowed never to speak of again in the family. It involved a horse, a fairground, a tea caddy and a lack of imagination.

It had started out innocently enough. It involved the two very large permanent fairgrounds which were open from Easter to the end of the summer holidays in September. They were magical places on even the dullest of days. That heady smell of candy floss and hot dogs, and the sulphuric smell of damp steam and hot oil from the little train which chugged around the marine lake, were all sensually hypnotic.

With money in your pocket you could sample the delights of the vintage gambling machines with polished Indian heads and tumblers which clicked out your fruity fate at the pull of the substantial steel handle. You could ride the dodgems like an electrified banshee and scream to hide your fear on the Ghost Train. In the hall of mirrors you could fracture your nose as you lost patience and headed for what you presumed was the exit. The only ride I was indifferent to was the horses.

The horses were corralled in a wooden pen under the roller-coaster and, on paying your sixpence, you got to ride the nags along a circuitous route that took you up a ramp, turned back on itself and continuously rose and fell until you arrived back at the starting point at the pen. The poor old horses looked bored to distraction and occasionally amused themselves by biting the punters or nuzzling up against the rail at the highest section of the walkway, leaving you pinned precariously over a drop of thirty feet by your leg, though the full weight of the malevolent horse ensured that you were more likely to crush your calf than fall to your death in a flurry of horse droppings.

I had some sympathy for the horses and would often stand close to the stall when some unsuspecting and over-enthusiastic girl holiday-maker rushed up to stroke the 'lovely horses', only to be turned upon by a cantankerous and foul-breathed beast meting out a substantial bite on the arm. How we laughed at this predictable spectacle and the look of hurt surprise on the victim's face.

I think if I had been made to stand around all day, with an awning ensuring I had no direct sunlight and steadily accumulating the slurry of horse manure underfoot, I too would have resorted to unprovoked acts of violence.

The delicately painted names on the bridles wouldn't have helped, that is assuming the horses could appreciate the lack of imagination of the grubby owner of the stall who had named the white horse Silver, the black one Blackie and the one that was neither white nor black, Dobbin. The brown one was Chestnut and the little Shetland pony, Tiny. I think the horses did suspect the lack of imagination in the naming policy, and this contributed to their generally disgruntled demeanour.

I did not even like riding the horses, which makes what followed all the more ironic.

It was the style that year to hang around with Ronnie. And Ronnie would be engaged in anything that impressed, or brought him into contact with Debbie, the new and good looking girl who smelt of Lux soap and had moved in three doors up from us.

As Debbie loved horses, every available day saw us trail to the fair, saddle up and take the reluctant horses for one more stroll around their prison yard. This could involve a considerable number of rides. As, in a good week, I only received pocket money to the sum of one shilling, at thruppence a ride I was soon out of pocket and risking being out of favour. Where to find a supply of thrupenny bits?

As luck would have it, there was a ready supply of thrupenny bits in the gloomy pantry under our stairs, which served as a stone-cold refrigerator. They were secreted away in an old tea caddy, which had been a long-ago visiting present from a former friend of my mum's. She had, at the end of the war, stolen mum's boyfriend and emigrated to Australia, having intercepted a silk dressing gown that the aforementioned boyfriend had sent to my mum via the errant.

The tea caddy was by way of a belated apology when the friend had turned up on our doorstep one day several years later, on a pilgrimage to the old country with her Australian children. My mum had greeted her warmly and had accepted the gift of the tea caddy with good grace, considering it was a rather poor substitute for one stolen boyfriend and a misappropriated silk dressing gown friend (not that my mum was bitter at the memory).

The tea caddy was undoubtedly tainted and it was not surprising, given its pedigree, that it should have been the source of my undoing.

To be precise, it was the use to which the tea caddy was put that caused 'the incident'. In order to gather funds in a not too ambitious way, my parents had taken to placing any thrupenny bits garnered in change into the tea caddy at the end of the day. Every few months, my father, who was good with figures, would count up the coins and bag them in the substantial green paper bags that the bank supplied for the purpose. The coins would be piled into fours, the fours counted into twenties and deposited in the bags which would be neatly and securely folded down to secure their precious cargo.

Every three months, coinciding with the week my father was on night shift he would take the bags to the Trustee Savings Bank and receive a signature and a credit when the bags had been tallied on the scales.

The tea caddy was such an easy target. As the change was deposited randomly, a few coins removed would not be detected and could not, therefore, be missed. Had I confined my pilfering to this scale, then I might never have been detected.

However, my new found ability to finance my horse riding attracted the attention of my riding companions. It was now they who were struggling to finance their passion and, in a display of largesse, I began to subsidise their riding habit. So deep was my generosity that I realised that the ever diminishing stash of coins in the tea caddy was looking decidedly impoverished and I resorted to making little raids into the bagged coins, carefully replacing the tab in the secure manner I had seen my father perfect.

At first, I kept a tally of which bags I had removed a single coin from but before long each had had a substantial weight removed from them. I longed for a long, cold, wet spell which would take us from our now daily visits to the fair, but the sun was a reluctant partner that year and conspired to shine on inappropriately each day of that long hot summer. By now my friends had come to expect me to pay for their ride, which only compounded the problem. I didn't have the heart or bottle to deny them. I remember practising my defence for when I was inevitably detected... that I had brought a lot of happiness to my friends by my action and that I did not profit directly myself. It did not prove a very convincing excuse as I rehearsed it, much less so when the inevitable came to pass.

It hurt greatly that, when it was finally discovered that there was money missing from the tea caddy, my parents tried to rationalise it because they did not believe I could have done such a thing. I was aching to tell them the truth but could not find the words to admit to stealing – as much to protect their high opinion of me as to protect myself. But when my dad returned from the bank on the fateful day having tried to palm off underweight one pound bags of coins I knew the game was up and the opportunity to make a clean breast of it had evaporated.

There were harsh words behind the closed front room door followed by a terrible silence. The fact that they had entered the hallowed front room to discuss my fate gave me a measure of the gravity of the situation.

I stood waiting for the storm that would begin my interrogation between the living room and the pantry, the scene of my misdemeanours. When the door finally opened I had steeled myself for every outcome but the one that transpired. My mum breezed past me and asked me if I wanted a drink.

The day proceeded in the same vein, and as, for once, the sun had decided not to show his face, I was confined to the house as the rain poured outside and compounded my misery. By night-time, I was pleased to seek an early refuge in my warm wincyetted bed. I knew that tomorrow would bring the inevitable show down but at least I could grab a few fitful hours sleep before then.

Tomorrow came, and the next day, without any outward sign of impending rage. And so we limped on to Saturday, the traditional pocket money day. By now, my worry had diminished but it persisted like dull tooth ache. At eight thirty when we were all gathered in the living room my mum reached into her hand bag, pulled out her blue leather purse which had been a present from Blackpool and handed me a silver half crown. I was about to return it when they both looked at me with a knowing stare.

"You only have to ask if you need money," my mum said.

I turned and ran out of the room, so deep was my humiliation.

It was a lesson I was never to forget and probably went some way towards my inability to accomplish my mission in Barton's.

Chapter Seven
STATION

Given the turbulence at times on the Reso, it is hardly surprising that everyone needed a place to retreat. For many, that involved fishing or bird egging or even the slot arcades on the promenade, but for me the place of retreat was the railway station.

The railway station was a place of magic and promise. The endless procession of black engines with their maroon coaches stopping briefly before moving on to destinations which promised so much, London Euston, calling at Crewe, Stafford, Nuneaton, Rugby and Watford Junction; or Holyhead, calling at Abergele, Colwyn Bay, Llandudno Junction (change for Deganwy and Llandudno), Conway, Llanfairfechan, Penmaenmawr and Bangor.

The sultry, female voice that announced them made them sound so sunny and enticing. I could never understand why the passengers, glimpsed through moving picture windows, did not show the same enthusiasm for their journey and their destinations. They sat, indifferent, staring blankly back or engrossed in newspapers or conversation, whilst I dreamt of the gilded far off city of gold that was Nuneaton.

They shuttled off to be replaced by their clones on the subsequent train fifteen minutes later.

On a summer's day you could look west down the line for a mile or so and when the sturdy semaphore arm was raised to inform you of the imminent arrival of the next train, you could see it indistinctly as it hove into view, shimmering in a heat haze which gave it a mirage-like quality.

It shimmied forth, becoming more distinct until we could recognise the class of engine, and finally it breasted the platform wheezing and clanking and hissing steam, revealing its prized number and drawing to a halt.

Usually, it would stop underneath the road bridge, and the steam and smoke would ricochet back off the bridge and we would stand there drinking in the sulphurous dampness. We'd be sure to be there as the train departed, when the steam cocks were opened to overcome the inertia, the cylinders burst into life, and the wheels spun in their efforts to grip the rails.

Between arrival and departure, we would ingratiate ourselves with the driver and the fireman, standing plaintively at the cabside trying to look endearing and responsible, which would be quite a difficult double act for some of us to pull off. For some trainspotters there was the more direct approach, "Cab yer Mister?". If the driver had a pleasant disposition and was not running against time the cab door would be opened and we would be beckoned aboard.

I have never ceased in my admiration for the crew of steam engines, coaxing into life some iron monster with nothing more than coal and water, and taming it to their bidding. The heat and noise were horrendous to us, but then a lever would be thrown to reveal an orange furnace, roaring with insistent, vibrant, volcanic fire and the fireman would hurl another round of coal into the firebox.

The driver would talk to us above this mechanical cacophony, showing us the controls, and it never occurred to us to stop him telling us what the previous driver had told us just twenty minutes ago, such was the enduring magic of the footplate. When the signal was pulled off to indicate the train's departure time, we would climb down and salute the crew, hoping they would remember us as 'good lads' and invite us on board next time.

Once we had alighted from the cab they returned to their more serious business and, with a wave and a shrill blast of the whistle, the underside of the bridge would explode in steam, noise and motion as the dragon resumed her labours, sucking in air and exhaling steam and smoke. Past went the tender with its smudged heraldic crest, past went the luggage compartment with the guard hanging out of the open door and then the carriages full of indifferent occupants. As each carriage passed, the de dum de dum of the bogies on the railjoints became more insistent. The last carriage passed, accelerating under the bridge and away to the romance that was Rugby. The signal bounced back to danger and the station returned to momentary silence.

Across the four tracks of the mainline was the platform for passengers travelling westwards along the coast, some assorted platform buildings with the distinctive verandahed roofs and beyond them the sidings and the coal yard, with its assortment of grime and corrugated buildings in a uniformly drab grey-black colour.

Each of the numerous signals around the station was a secret code, like a computer selecting channels of communication. Large red signals with vertical white stripes and yellow signals with a black chevron like medieval banners trumpeted the arrival of the important visitors. Small fussy ground signals, no more than red and white discs, indicating routes of minor importance and all linked to the mysterious movement of the points which changed the direction and ultimate destination of the trains in the same way that decisions we make determine our route through life.

All this could be had on any day of the week for the princely sum of two old pennies, deposited with a reassuring clunk in the red and cream platform ticket machine at the ticket office, except Sunday, which was a barren railway day. We could, of course, have sneaked onto the platform for free from a number of secret entrances, but that would have been to risk expulsion and the inevitable ignominy of the ticket collector reminding you that he, "knew your Dad!".

Far more profitable to be able legitimately to proffer one's platform ticket for inspection, trying to imagine that it was a real ticket and could take you on a steam-powered fantasy journey to Deganwy or even beyond.

In the lull between trains there were numerous distractions. Daring to go into the Gentlemen's urinals was a favourite as they were fabled to be populated with rats, which, if cornered, would leap unerringly for your throat. I always went to the toilet before going to the station.

Near the passenger bridge which connected the two platforms was a stamping machine that took thin billets of aluminium and allowed you to imprint letters in it via the mechanism of a huge clock face of letters, spaces and punctuation marks. So much fun for a penny! You selected your letter then pulled down on a large handle to punch it into the metal. The reason for having this machine escapes me and I never knew anyone but us to use it. Having made all variations of our names in metal, our thoughts turned inevitably to rude words. I once managed to get 'bum titty bum bu' out of the machine before my allotted letters ran out, and three of us sat laughing until we cried on the cold stone slabs of the platform.

There was a WHS kiosk on the platform manned, or rather womanned, by a person with hawkish eyes and manner, who always wore a scarf and a dirty nylon overall. She was one of my nain's generation, and always had a cigarette on. The cigarette never left her mouth and the ash would hang on as she talked, transacted sales and viewed us with suspicion.

The front of the kiosk had newspapers and magazines held in place against errant winds and rushing trains by the same plastic coated wire that held up the net curtains at home.

At each end of the kiosk were glass fronted display cases which remained unchanged in all the time I remember them. In one of these were books and annuals including the Bible of the serious trainspotter, 'The Ian Allen Combined Volume' which listed all the locomotives and shed codes across the land. At ten shillings and sixpence (52p), this was way beyond our means. We had to put up with a series of notepads and little ledger books which were inevitably lost or purloined by mums for shopping lists.

In the display case at the other end of the kiosk, on a sun-faded piece of sugar paper of the sort we used for art in school, was an enticing, if rather old, display of chocolate boxes. We assumed the boxes were empty as the chocolates would have melted by now in the summer sun. But the Meltis jelly fruit segments box might still be inhabited as they, we assumed, would not melt. One box of chocolates had been removed quite recently as the space it occupied was of a significantly darker shade then the straw shade of the rest of the display. The only sign of recent movement in the display were the two dead wasps which had no doubt crawled in to investigate the contents of the Meltis jelly fruit segments box, and had died in the attempt.

Behind the woman were at least ninety glass jars containing varying quantities of every imaginable sweet. Much as the wine gums, dolly mixtures and treacle toffee appealed, the idea of the dirty, nicotine-stained hands of the hawk woman handling the confectionery into the scales and coughing and dropping fag ash over them as she leaned forward to squint and read the weight, always put me off buying loose sweets there.

John suggested we play a trick on the woman, based on a joke his dad had told him. We should ask the woman for a quarter of wasps, pointing at the array of glass jars that held such enticing confectionery. When she said she didn't sell wasps we'd all reply, "Then why have you got two on display in your window?!" and again we were off in uncontrollable fits of laughter at the thought of the look on her face. In such ways we passed the time between trains.

In the summer months these interludes were short, as Rhyl was a holiday resort, and in the days before widespread car ownership the train was the favoured method of holiday traffic. Add to this the single day excursion of the type I longed to enjoy, and there was an endless procession of trains queuing for space at the platforms. The semaphores were ceaselessly animated, announcing the imminent arrival of trains from foreign parts – well, foreign parts as far as I was concerned.

These were golden trainspotting opportunities as the occasional maroon and green Coronation Class engines with majestic smoke deflectors would be interspersed with the mundane Black Fives.

The excursion trains brought unusual engines from far away places such as Nottingham, Leicester and the Birmingham suburbs, and the occupants for once would have the same sort of animation I would bring to such a journey. They would be gaudily dressed for the seaside and would spill onto the platforms like rainbows.

They held a fascination for us, as we could not see the attraction of coming to our home town as a treat. We lived there and it had no special appeal to us – how wretched their lives must be to be able to consider a visit to us as a holiday.

Chapter Eight
HAUNTED

I tended to pick my friends to suit the occasion. I had football friends for whom being hard was not as important as being skilled – and having the most skilful player on your side – and I had other knocking-about friends who would be determined by the nature of the activity in hand. By choosing my friends carefully, I could enjoy such things as trainspotting and, at the same time, keep in with friends who made me feel pretty hard. Others worked the same system and I was usually somewhere in the pecking order of my other friends - except when the subject turned to going on a bike ride, where I was deficient to the tune of one bicycle.

It was, however, a mistake to mix friends and different activities, and I made the slip-up one day of inviting Ronnie to come trainspotting. It must have been a particularly slow day because he agreed and we made our way to a favourite spot of mine at the far end of the large sandstone H bridge where we could see either way down the track as we waited for the arrival of a train – westwards along the coast or eastwards into the throat of the station.

It felt like a Sunday as the pace of the train activity was slow. We entertained ourselves with the usual fare of boy games – who could withstand the Chinese burn, arm-wrestling and throwing ears of grass like arrows into our jumpers.

Within half an hour we were scraping the barrel and had turned to True, Dare, Kiss, Command or Promise. This was usually only played in mixed company to heighten the tension of the Kiss forfeit but it demonstrated how disillusioned Ronnie had become with trainspotting. I always veered to the True as I was quite happy to listen to any insult heaped on me or my family, knowing this was only a game.

After three rounds of Ronnie doing his worst on my True forfeit, this, by the way, included us eating rabbit droppings on toast for tea, being related to the Barkers and my wearing my mum's cast-me-down knickers, Ronnie said I had to choose another forfeit.

Reluctantly I went for the Dare, knowing that a failure to comply with the forfeit would have Ronnie labelling me a chicken on the estate. The stakes were suddenly raised and Ronnie cast around for a suitably ludicrous forfeit. I had a feeling it would involve the railway tracks and running across when the train was approaching. I had a real problem with this, for as well as it being patently stupid, I didn't want to be asking those same drivers that I had terrified the day before, if I could cab them the next day. It didn't seem right, and no amount of claiming to be a foreign visitor with a lunatic look-alike would cover up for that sort of stupidity.

To my surprise Ronnie's gaze went in the opposite direction, to the Witch's House. He'd thought up an equally unpalatable forfeit.

For as long as anyone could remember the shaded house which stood alone behind the bridge had been known as the Witch's House. Even my mum and dad had known it as that in their childhood. The house had all the classic ingredients. The garden was hideously overgrown, with a rusted lawn roller swallowed up by the weeds and brambles. A wooden picket fence had faded to dinginess and a hawthorn bush had burst through it.

The house itself was detached and, had it been painted white and well kept, would have passed as a desirable family house. As it was, at least two generations of neglect had bleached it to an almost uniform grey, relieved only by the stucco pebble-dashing, which had growing patches of green, damp mould. Bramble had invaded the walls and had even begun to obscure the windows of the bedrooms, giving the house the feeling of being reclaimed by the earth.

All the windows were dirty and had intricately patterned, though fading, nets and heavy dark curtains in them. The net curtains were spoilt in some rooms and had tears in them, where, so it was said, some of the witch's victims had tried to escape.

I had never seen the witch, but then again you wouldn't, would you? You'd hardly see her down the local shops buying a packet of fags, the paper and some milk for her cat. When trainspotting, we'd stare at the house for ages trying to see any sign of life. We decided to keep on staring one morning until we saw the witch take in a milk bottle. We'd been on the task for almost an hour when the shuffling of points and the raising of a signal alerted us to the imminent arrival of an express and, in the brief time we were distracted by its passing, the milk disappeared from the doorstep.

The only movement we ever observed was the slight ruffling of the curtains – strangely this seemed to occur simultaneously in several rooms which further freaked us out. Had the witch developed some strange spookish contraption that could move curtains in several rooms at once? Or was there more than one witch in the house – or even one witch who could be in more than one room at the same time? All the permutations seemed equally diabolical.

The only movement we could definitely vouch for was of the witch's cat – a malevolent, traditional black cat with jaundiced yellow eyes. The cat never ventured beyond the garden but had an unnatural authority in its own territory. We would make loud tomcat meows designed to panic it, and it would merely look back knowingly at us. It taunted us, so we threw gravel at it – never managing to hit it and never moving it from its spot. "Come on in – if you think you are hard enough," it seemed to say.

Ronnie had obviously heard the cat as well, as his Dare was to go to the Witch's House and knock on the door, then stand at the gate until she opened it. Needless to say, I declined and had to live with the tag 'chicken' for a number of weeks. In fact, at times of dispute, Ronnie would always bring up this subject and, whenever it was my turn to Dare, I would give him the same Dare.

He would say, "No returns," and that I could not give a Dare that I had passed on, and we descended into one of those...

"Did!"

"Didn't!"

"Could!"

"Couldn't!" type of arguments until we both fell silent through boredom, or Ronnie got in, "and no comebacks!" before me.

Up until now all I have said about the Witch's House I know to be true because I witnessed it, but what I am about to tell you is a story my mum told me a few years later, after we had moved from the estate. Whether it is true or not I cannot say, but it would not have been out of keeping with the reputation of the house.

I'd asked her why we had not bought our own house when we had moved off the Reso and this launched her into this tale which both engrossed and horrified me....

One day, some time after the witch had moved, somebody, with greater courage than I had mustered, did enter the garden. They went in with a long wooden stake and drove it into the overgrown lawn, scaring off the cat in the process. To this stake they attached a sign, a bright coloured sign, the brightest thing that garden had seen in many a long year. The sign read… *For Sale.*

What had happened to the witch remains unclear. She may have moved on, or vanished, or maybe she had just died all alone, as little old ladies sometimes do. Perhaps the local people felt ashamed of the way they had treated a lonely old woman, and perhaps they didn't.

Within weeks, the house had been sold to an ambitious family with two young children, who saw the 'potential' of it, and set aside a considerable sum in order to gut it and start refurbishing it from the ground up.

In the following weeks, a succession of workmen exorcised the dark spirit of the gloomy old house, ripping things out, sawing, cutting and smashing until a pall of dust hung round its entrails. The rendering was removed and replaced. The windows repainted and slowly the house took on a different look. The picket fence was substituted by iron railings, once the succession of lorries had delivered building supplies across the lawn.

A month later the family moved in. They were left with a great deal of painting to do. Each morning, the husband would leave in his suit for work. Each evening he would return, get changed, and begin an evening's painting and decorating.

The wife was equally hard working. Having taken the children through the fed, read and bed routine, she too would embark on some painting. In this way many evenings passed and the house was slowly transformed.

My mother explained that the local population had mixed feelings about the change. On the one hand, they lamented the end of yet another local landmark. On the other hand, they were very impressed with the way the house was coming back to life.

One Friday night the husband returned home, donned his work clothes and set about one of the upstairs rooms. This routine was wearing a little thin by now. The constant smell of paint and the endless cleaning brushes was driving him to distraction. Within an hour the children had been settled down and his wife had joined him, stripping wallpaper in an adjacent room.

"This wall hasn't been stripped since the house was built !" she called from her room. "You've got the decorating tastes of four generations here."

And so the evening passed, with snippets of conversation and much frantic activity. At ten o'clock the husband leaned back from the skirting board, nursed his aching back and declared, "I'm bushed, that's me finished for the night, make us a milky drink, love!"

He dragged himself downstairs, cleaned out his brush in the pungent-smelling turpentine and collapsed on the sofa with the television blaring out the news.

Soon his wife joined him with two milky coffees and a packet of chocolate digestive biscuits.

For ten minutes they ate and drank before sinking motionless in that half awake coma that the television induces.

At this point, to develop the drama of the scene, my mother stopped and stared vacantly for a few seconds before continuing.

After what seemed like minutes, she continued impressively, but could have been hours, the husband awoke to the distinct smell of burning. He nudged his half comatose wife and said," I think you've left the milk pan on the stove, love."

"No, I put it in the sink," she replied sleepily.

But now the smell reached her nostrils too and she leapt up and shot into the kitchen to find it as she had left it. Gas off and pan soaking in the sink. Her husband joined her and they tried to locate the burning smell, through the kitchen, into the hallway and upwards they went onto the landing. The smell was becoming stronger now and their sense of fear was growing. The husband was replaying the evening events to find a point at which he could have done something that could have lead to a fire. No blowlamps, no brushes with electricity. He could think of nothing that could have done so.

As they stood on the landing their worst fears materialised. At the top of the flight of stairs leading to the attic was a flickering, cherry red glow. Further investigation revealed that it was coming from under the attic room door.

"How could this be?" my mother asked rhetorically as I stared open mouthed and without an answer.

The door to that room had remained stubbornly locked since they had moved in. They had thought of breaking down the door but the quality of the door was so good they had decided to leave it as a future project for when the rest of the house was complete. The room had remained undisturbed, so how could it now be on fire?

In the time they had taken to think this through, a thick pall of yellow-brown acrid smoke had begun to billow out from under the door and make its way down the stairs towards them. With a concerted scream, they rushed into the children's room and dragged them from their beds. Wrapping them in their duvets, they carried them half sleeping and half protesting, downstairs and into the garden.

My mother was speaking quickly now, driving the story along at a frenetic pace.

They had stood terrified, looking up at the red glow from the attic, the smoke billowing out of a crack in the window. They were panic-stricken. All their dreams and all their money were tied up in this house – to lose it now would ruin them.

Unable to contain himself, the husband ran back into the house, despite his wife's protests. He burst into the kitchen, dampened a tea towel which he wrapped about his mouth and nose, and made his way up the stairs to investigate the source of the fire.

What he thought he could do at this stage is debateable. He was beyond reason and motivated by sheer panic. It was the thought of the ruination this fire would cause the family that drove him on.

As he mounted the stairs, the heat, and above all, the thick, acrid, foul smelling smoke came down to meet him. This smoke was almost animal like, clawing the air around him and forcing its way into his eyes and nostrils. It had the consistency of the coils of a snake, and an abrasive quality that tore the lining off the inside of his nostrils leaving him weak and breathless.

He began to feel the life being extinguished from him and still he drove on up the stairs to the pulsating red glow emanating from under the attic room door. His progress was now faltering and his body leaden. Through his squinting eyes, he could just make out the door knob glowing red, and at this point, his body began to relax into submission. As his senses began to depart and he lapsed into darkness, he was roused by the shriek and cackle of some demonic beast, loud and close, and amused by his imminent demise.

My mother had slowed the story to a shuffle now, limping forward, hinting at the uncertainty. The banshee howl she now let out stunned me with its intensity.

In a second, time was reversed and the smoke retraced its course as if Hoovered back into the attic room. The pulsating fire departed and the house was reduced to silence.

My mother licked her lips at this point and I felt my Adam's apple bounce as I took in more air.

Draped over five stairs, our hero lay motionless, desperately trying to unscramble his thoughts. He opened his eyes slowly and had all his senses check in before he dared move. He drew in several lungfuls of air and toyed with the idea that he had died.

Slowly, he gathered himself up and moved carefully to the attic door. He quickly touched the doorknob – expecting to be burnt. He found it cool to the touch.

He grabbed it and turned it. Unlike previous occasions, it gave way, and the door slowly yielded with a creaking of hinges.

My mother did not have to imitate the creaking of the hinges as I heard it as if I was a witness at the scene.

He squinted again, hardly daring to see what horrors the room concealed. The door was fully open now and his eyes gazed on a truly amazing site – an empty room. Empty and fragrant. A set of pristine floorboards, bare walls with floral wallpaper and a few lighter coloured areas where once had hung pictures, and everywhere the scent of roses.

But in the furthest corner, high up on the wall sat... a small spider busily spinning its web. Except for that, the room was empty and seemed undisturbed.

The man took several deep breaths in an effort to clear his head and make some sense of the bizarre events. He could not and simply retreated out of the room and down the stairs, where he was met by his wife.

"What has happened?" she demanded.

"I don't know," he replied. "I suggest we get some sleep, we've obviously been overdoing it."

They slept fitfully that night and in the morning he began to recount what he thought had been a dream from the night before, but it was clear from her reaction that this was more than a dream.

My mother was back to her matter of fact voice now and I had many questions unanswered. I dare not interrupt the flow of the story though.

They replayed the events of the night before, trying to reach some logical explanation, without success: fumes from the paint, an optical illusion? Nothing seemed to fit. In the end they accepted that they had been a party to some very strange and inexplicable events. Though neither considered themselves religious, having carefully eliminated all other explanations, they were left with a supernatural one. Karen, somewhat against her better judgement, was left to telephone the local vicar to seek his advice.

She was rather surprised at his matter of fact reaction to her story.

"The night before last you say? Why yes, of course, the full moon. Fear not dear lady. I think I have the solution to your unpleasant predicament. I shall contact you anon. Or rather on the evening of the twenty first of next month."

Karen was both reassured and concerned by the vicar's attitude. How could such strange events produce such a response? It seemed no more alarming to the vicar than a phone call to arrange a christening. Perhaps there was more of this sort of activity than one might think, mused Karen.

It was, none the less, something of a surprise when the vicar appeared at the door at eight p.m. precisely on the evening of the twenty first. Karen's first reaction was to reach for her purse as she assumed the vicar had come in pursuit of funds for the parish appeal – things must be desperate for him to be out this late on such a stormy evening – but a quick conversation cleared up the misunderstanding and the soaking vicar was brought into the warmth of the house.

He was a thin and well presented man with a narrow face and light blue eyes which seemed to be ever focused on the face of whomever he was listening to. It was quite unnerving to be met by his intense gaze and, although the mouth smiled, the eyes always seemed to penetrate the surface of things.

He was most interested in the layout of the house and the focus of the previous month's incident. Karen and Martin were as open as they could be when discussing the events of that night. The vicar cross-examined them quite intently until at last he was satisfied. He stroked his chin and drew in a long breath. They waited for him to exhale. He seemed to use this lungful of air to power some inner process and finally exhaled equally deeply.

I tried to mimic the vicar but did not have the lung capacity to hold my breath for any significant time and my mother was keen to move the story forward. She leant forward and with a vicar's gravity continued...

"I can remove this burden from the house this evening. I must set up post on the top landing," he stated.

Karen and Martin were both taken aback by this statement but, bowing to his superior knowledge of such matters, agreed to make him comfortable on the top landing with a high-backed armchair, supply of hot chocolate, assorted biscuits, a rug and a lamp, and a tot of whisky. As he settled into the chair, he reached into the black bag which until now had gone unnoticed by Martin and Karen. In the light from the shaded lamp at the side of the chair, Martin made out a glint of silver metal – a cross with ornamental carving. There seemed to be a wide range of unusual objects in the bag, but the vicar was intent on delving to the bottom for the most hidden of them all. They were both surprised when the cleric finally pulled out a rather battered copy of an Agatha Christie novel – but this was not before he had mistakenly pulled out an equally battered copy of the Bible and replaced it carefully in the bag.

"That's me sorted," he declared and pulled the travel rug around his legs.

"Whatever happens later, don't be alarmed – the fireworks come with the territory."

With the Reverend happily tucked in on the top landing, and onto his third tot of whisky, they retired to bed. It felt strange trying to fall off to sleep, with the vicar sitting above them on the little landing, waiting to do who knows what to God knows what, and it was some time before their idle chatting descended into the heavy and rhythmic pattern of sleep.

The whole house grew quiet with only the occasional creak from the stairs and the hum of the refrigerator. An orb of pearl light glowed around the reading vicar on the high landing. Outside, the air was still and heavy, and the full moon struggled through layers of dense, broken cloud which diffused its glow, accentuating the eerie light from the streetlamps. And so the minutes ticked on uneventfully, and from the bedroom of the owners of the house the laboured breathing began to subside into snoring.

My mother had slowed to an awfully ominous pace and I suspected something shrill was about to occur...

"AAAAAIIIIEEEEE!" A demonic scream shattered the night and simultaneously, Martin and Karen were jolted out of their slumbers to hear the reasoned tones of the vicar speaking as to some agitated Alsatian, "Well, you are a big beast aren't you? Back to where you've come from my beauty!"

In a fearful replay of events one month before, the bedroom was now aglow with that same red eeriness that had coloured the previous nightmare. Martin and Karen were up and at the bedroom door in an instant.

In their rapid movement to support the vicar, they were aware of the open attic room door and the outline of the vicar's dark clothes silhouetted against a fearful red light. Within the light was the outline of some beast, huge, muscular and, even from this distance, foul smelling. A stench of sulphur, of burning and decay - a smell which instantly dampened the spirits and drenched them in a fearful depression that slowed all movement and feeling.

Clasping each other's hands for encouragement, they slowly moved forward – too slowly for the vicar though, for, as if levitated, he was vacuumed into the room whose door now slammed shut with such force that the whole landing shook.

I could feel my own heart racing now as my mother pressed on to the terrible conclusion...

There were screams and the pulsating glow of red light at the doorknob and beneath the door. As before, the pungent, yellow brown cloud began to uncoil down the stairs to confront them, serpent - like and mesmeric in its movement.

Martin drew back, knowing that their combined efforts would have no effect on the outcome of this confrontation. Martin had no wish to have a second encounter with the force contained within that acrid cloud.

In an instant the commotion subsided and the cloud withdrew, sinewy and sly.

The redness disappeared and only the vicar's lamp illuminated a scene of terrible normality. In the background, the refrigerator continued to hum, the clock to tick, and Martin and Karen to breathe heavily.

It was Martin who moved first, slowly approaching the door, hesitation in his every movement. Karen waited on the stairs unable to move forwards or retreat in the shocking aftermath of these events.

Martin touched the doorknob, so recently glowing red. It was cool to the touch and yielded easily when turned. He pushed open the door which made that classic horror story creak as it yielded – only this was no cheap film – this was their house.

He beckoned Karen up and she took each step deliberately, as if testing both the stairs and her courage. They stood at the entrance to the room only to find it empty, slightly dusty, cool, the moon now streaming through the window, having chased away the clouds.

Looking deep into my eyes, I sensed my mother was going to share the secret of the house and I craned forward....

They took a step forward and saw behind the door the only sign of the titanic struggle which had so recently taken place.

On its side on the floorboards was the vicar's left shoe. Smoke was rising from it, and the tainted odour of burned flesh was all around.

Burned deep in the sole of the shoe was a sign, a symbol, some writing which could only be deciphered when the shoe was turned to face the light of the moon. On the sole of the shoe were burned the words...

Stead and Simpson, Size 7.

"And that," stated my mum, suddenly jolting the image, "is why we will not be buying our own house but will continue renting from the council. They've got an environmental health department to deal with problems like this. You never know what you are taking on when you buy a house." She'd done it again.

Chapter Nine
VISITORS

Trains from Birmingham also brought thick nasal accents with them, like our new neighbours, the Waltons, who had made this journey countless times and had decided to settle in the town of so many holiday memories with fresh air and fresh fish.

One particular family caught my eye, as they were last to leave the train and seemed to show less enthusiasm for the day than the rest of the army of passengers. Either something had been lost on route or the boy among the party, who insisted on wearing an inflated tractor tyre around his waist, had prevented an easy exit from the carriage. He popped onto the platform, followed by a dowdy girl whose bright floral dress was not in keeping with her sullen and pasty face.

Mother came next with fat arms and a substantial black handbag followed by father with ruddy complexion and the obvious impression that he was on a Sunday outing, as he was wearing his best suit set off with sandals and threadbare black workaday socks. He carried his grey suit jacket over his arm and panted for breath, mopping his sweating brow with a white handkerchief.

They seemed over-dressed both for the occasion and the weather, for this was one of the hottest weekends of the year and I had been delayed on my way to the station to stick lollipop sticks in the tar bubbles which were forming in the road.

Intrigued by what I saw as a debacle in the making, I chose to follow this particular family out of the station and up the High Street onto the beach.

It was a favourite misconception of families that lived far away from the coast, and in Birmingham in particular, that the sea was a sort of unconstrained swimming pool. Such dangerous ideas were often of high amusement value to us who lived by it and knew its dangers, and also the location of the sewage outlet pipes. The fact that this lad, overweight and clueless, had brought an inflated tractor tyre with him heightened the expectation of imminent disaster. Imminent disaster for him, entertainment for us.

Inevitably, his acquaintance with the sea would entail the firing of the maroons, huge rocket fireworks which boomed above the town to call the lifeboat crew to muster, the launch of the lifeboat and the possibility of the arrival of the yellow RAF rescue helicopter – all entertainment provided free by an idiot with a tractor tyre. Too good an opportunity to forego, even on an excursion filled summer Saturday.

The only problem was the time it would take them to get to the beach. The High Street was no more than half a mile long but here were so many shopping distractions for urban dwellers. Tacky souvenir stalls with plastic merchandise in all shapes and colours, 'authentic' rock shops in which rock could be bought in all forms and flavours, most ironically in the shape of a pair of false teeth, which is what would be required should you ingest the volume of processed sugar that made up these awful gnashers. Candy floss like beehive hair-dos, and toffee apples vied for your taste buds – all artificial, all superficial. The candy floss melted to sugary nothing in your mouth but proved incredibly persistent if it stuck to clothing or your fingers – as it would without fail in the wind or the jostling crowds.

The cafeteria situated two thirds up the length of the High Street would always pull them in, with parents gasping for a cup of tea and a scone with jam and cream. A reproduction of a cream tea was set out in the window and it never failed to win over punters. For this was what the holidaymakers were to the local business people – punters. People who should be parted from their money by the fastest and most efficient means possible whilst sun, sand and sea breezes worked their magic and loosened their wallets – for who can smell the sea air without thinking fish and chips, hot dogs, rock, candy floss, tacky souvenirs and cream teas?

Of course, the children would bitterly resent this intrusion on their beach time and would become sullen and uncooperative – setting the tone for the rest of the day.

Surprisingly, the next port of call was always Woolworths, which was the last stop before the beach. I am sure the inhabitants of Dudley, Halesowen and Redditch had their own Woolworths, selling exactly the same merchandise, but the fact that this one was practically on the beach made it continental and exotic. You could imagine the Mum showing holiday snaps in the hairdressers the following week and pointing out, "This is us going into their Woolworths. It's much the same as ours on the inside but theirs is practically on the Beach!"

"On the beach - fancy that! How continental!" would be the riposte from the gathered clientele.

The front doors of Woolworths opened out onto the Promenade where the habitual wind blended frying onions with ozone to create that unforgettable seaside smell.

The younger members of the family now faced a stark choice between two equally appealing attractions. To the left was the Golden Mile of slot arcades, raucous bingo callers and Kiss Me Quick hat stalls, ahead the home made dairy ices, the splendour of the Beach and the Sea.

Faced with the shoddy, brash commercialism of the arcades and the splendour of the Beach, they invariably chose the arcades. Here they would while away a couple of hours converting silver to bronze and bronze to losses in the constant delusion that the next penny in the slot would be the big winner. In the end, their palms would smell of damp pennies as the sweat flowed and the losses mounted.

To the beach then, peeved and skint but filled up with hot dogs with onions and mustard and toffee apples.

There was a last redoubt of soft commercialism as they approached the beach. A range of pleasant distractions run by sun-browned, amiable looking folk with hard, commercial outlooks.

There was a Punch and Judy Professor who would stand sullen and smoking beside his tall striped tent as the minutes ticked by to the time of the next show chalked on the small easel on the miniature stage:

Roll up Children, next show at 2.00 pm

The liverish, sharp eyed professor, at once despising and cajoling his clientele whilst taking sips of tea from his thermos. I never really got the Punch and Judy show. Like pantomime, I found it faintly alarming – a make believe world where adults confused children and took part in unspeakable acts of theatrical cruelty. I had little problem with the gaily coloured hedonist Mr Punch – a Sammy Barker look-alike and act-alike.

Mrs Punch, the domestic drudge with the hatchet nose reminded me of some of the mums on the estate who were never seen out of a pinafore and a headscarf. The dog, the sausages and the baby I was largely indifferent to but the Policeman and the Crocodile filled me with dread: the Policeman for reasons which will become clear later, the Crocodile for two wildly unconnected but equally frightening reasons. First there was the clack of those papier-mâché jaws which preceded the crocodile's appearance and always filled me with primal fear. Perhaps, in a previous life, I had been hunted down by a crocodile – fanciful but possible, but those snapping jaws evoked some terrible half memory of being pursued and being unable to escape that I simply could not shake off.

The other reason was very real, and recent. In the back of Mad Terrence's Science lesson I had chosen to amuse myself during his treatise on magnetism with an impromptu Punch and Judy show featuring a slat from one of the uncomfortable wooden chairs and a sock from my P.E. kit. The show was devised for the amusement of my back row colleagues – all of whom had by now lost interest in the lesson, whilst I was totally lost in the world of errant fathers, sausages and crying babies.

The play had started in muted tones so as not to alert the rest of the class, who were deeply involved in the opposites attract, likes repel, part of the talk. Unfortunately, the crescendo of my performance coincided with a lull in Mad Terrence's, and my shouting, "The Crocodile's got the sausages!" in a pretty good rendition of Mr Punch's voice was clearly heard across the room.

I glanced up from the magical world of puppetry to find the whole class turned looking at me. I hoped to rescue the situation with some comic riposte but could only manage, "You naughty Crocodile spoiling the lesson!" Unfortunately I forgot to drop Mr Punch's voice.

I glanced around the room and although I could see some of my classmates biting their tongue to stop themselves laughing out loud as their shoulders heaved up and down, I could not be sure if it was at my comic antics or the anticipation my impending doom.

In his characteristic economic style, Mad Terrence frowned and gestured me forward, with my comic creations. I gathered them up and made my way to the front of the class. The Science classroom was all wooden floors and benches, unchanged since the school had opened and I felt a little like Oliver Twist making his way towards Mr Bumble.

When I reached the raised dais from which Mad Terrence had been holding forth on the magical properties of magnets, he simply held out his hand. I handed over the slat and the sock. With his huge hands he took the slat and snapped it in two without the shadow of a grimace of effort on his face. He handed the two pieces and accompanying splinters to me and gestured for me to put them in the sock. He then bade me take the sock to the window and drop it out.

"I'm pleased to see that Hughes has found himself a career for which he is so clearly suited. I'm minded to dispense with his scholastic training completely, but perhaps we should keep him like some brainless jack in the box – to entertain us when we have completed our serious studies?"

I didn't know what it meant but it did not sound good and I was relieved at the end of the lesson when I managed to leave the classroom without a serious beating.

Our holidaymakers were only momentarily distracted by the Punch and Judy as a twenty-five minute wait in such an entertainment-rich environment was simply not on.

They were instead enticed by Uncle Walter's Children's Amusements. This comprised an area the size of a small car park with swings in the middle and a race track delineated by used railway sleepers painted in a variety of garish gloss paints.

Above these railway sleepers, suspended by sharp steel stanchions, at the height of 2ft 6 ins was a thin nylon rope to prevent punters straying into the course area. Many of the sleepers were cunningly disguised beneath windblown sand and at the far end of the arena was Uncle Walter, spider-like, an avaricious and malevolent ne'r-do-well who could barely raise a smile from his rat-like features.

For the sum of a sixpence you could hire one of Uncle Walter's vehicles for ten laps of the circuit. There were bicycles and tricycles of all sizes and those metal cars with pedals on which I'd always cut my knees. Most had a very efficient speed limiter insofar as the tyres, brakes and all other components were so badly worn and sand infiltrated that it was all you could do to make the wheels turn. However, each year Uncle Walter made the magnificent gesture of buying a single vehicle.

The last three years' vehicles were still in reasonable repair, so the local children, to whom Uncle Walter was slightly better disposed as he "Knew your Dad", would wait patiently for these to become available before proffering their sixpences.

The surface of the marked out track was treacherous – loose gravel ground to the consistency of sandpaper by the wind blown sand. The rules of the track were minimal and in essence involved only going round it in one way.

When we did not have a sixpence, the possibilities to watch a repeating drama unfold were limitless.

In choosing vehicles, the girls always went for the sedate options. There was a tricycle with a fur horse's head which was battered from abuse and rain, which proved very popular. For the boys, only the fastest vehicle would do and they were invariably drawn to the more serviceable of the bicycles.

The age range of the riders varied from four upwards and the strength of riders coupled to the dubious serviceability of the vehicles meant that a heady broth of pleasure seeking humanity would be moving in varying and erratic directions at the same time. It was an accident waiting to happen. Young children, moving one way and looking over their shoulders to keep their parents in view; girls talking and steering erratically as the conversation took them, and older boys, determined to set the fastest lap as they wound up the speed – their little legs a blur of furious peddling energy.

Slowly at first, and then quicker as the laps ticked off, they would build up the momentum of a coiled spring, past the tots on their tricycles, the girls deep in conversation, moving each lap to the less congested area at the outside of the track, all the time moving away from the well-worn, smooth tarmac to the rough, chipping spattered perimeter. A fast lap, legs off the pedals, they'd signal their parents, "Look no feet!".

A faster lap, "Look mum no hands!" and mum would glare back, urging caution.

And finally, at the height of the adrenalin, at the perimeter of the track, at the summit of their joy, they'd lose control of the bicycle. Their feet would be off the pedals and their new jelly shoes would find no resistance on the loose tarmac, their hands would grip the ineffectual brakes and their jaw would be clamped shut as if to influence the braking effectiveness.

For a second they'd appear to have stabilised the situation, but inevitably the front wheel would hit the sand and pull the bike into the railway sleeper, slewing the bike to the right while they continued straight on into an artless curve of sprawling arms and legs which made a long, drawn out impact with the merciless loose tarmac.

Along one side of their body they'd remain pristine but as they picked themselves up, hands held as if dripping wet, face actually dripping wet, the chippings would have extracted a terrible toll of skin and cloth. Whole areas would be red - grey and black as blood and tarmac merged.

Uncle Walter would race, as much as any sixty-year old could race, to the scene of the accident and carefully retrieve the bicycle, leading it back to the waiting queue, ready to re-enact the scene with new punters.

Mothers would be alerted and would appear like hens with a mixture of worry and anger. They would not know whether to cuddle or smack their irresponsible young ones and most decided to do both to be safe. The blubbering mass would be led away to the First Aid Post, stiff-legged, blubbing and wincing. Hardly had the noise of screaming subsided when the scrape of sandals on tarmac heralded the next victim.

A whole day's entertainment could be had in such ways with the routine crash punctuated by the over exuberant youngster on the tricycles failing to make the 180-degree turn at the far end of the track to be garrotted by the nylon rope that marked the perimeter of the track.

If they survived the mayhem that was Uncle Walter's, our holiday-making family, like turtles, had now made it to the sea.

For those who live there, the Beach is a treacherous place, to be treated with respect at all times. To holidaymakers it is an adventure playground.

The first mistake is to ignore the state of the tides. If you must swim, and there are strong arguments not to, including danger and raw sewage, swim only when the tide is coming in. For those cooped up in landlocked parts all year round, the excitement of exposure to the sea meant that even this rudimentary rule was broken – especially if you had gone to the trouble of lugging a tractor tyre from the suburbs of Brum.

And so the swimming trunk two step would begin as our loud and overweight hero attempted to change into his trunks on a crowded beach with the aid of a small towel which was somewhat short of covering his full circumference. He wobbled, hopping, exposing various bits of his anatomy as he tried to work his leg into his trunks. A whole beach of people tried desperately to look in the opposite direction, as a flabby moon cast its shadow across the sands.

When the tide had the temerity to go out he simply legged it out to meet it across vast acreages of uneven sand.

At its furthest point, which unbeknown to him was some twenty feet below the level at which the family were currently laying out the tablecloth for the picnic, the beach shelved. It shelved very gradually at first, so they would chase a further few hundred yards into the water before their feet no longer touched terra firma.

By now he was more than a mile from his parents and, when the combination of sea and wind was right this distance would soon be doubled and then doubled again. What is more, he was now tired from his exertions carrying the tyre over the beach and he would quickly be aware that the fuggy heat of the walk through town had now given way to a sharp and biting cold as the sweat off his body was replaced by tangy, freezing sea water.

For most, panic or exhaustion would now set in. Our boy, if he was observant, if his senses had not been dulled by the cold, might have noticed the strangely brown consistency of the water at this point, for he was currently floating amongst the liquid and solid detritus of his fellow holiday makers. This was where the contents of the sewage pipe created that rich faecal soup beloved of sea life: 95% brown floating masses to 5% clean sea water.

The parents, immersed in trying to recreate a genteel country garden party with a red rug, a thermos, a small parcel of hot and sweating egg sandwiches and a howling wind, were oblivious to the fate of their first born.

The sullen daughter, too self conscious to expose herself to the local view, sat immersed in a trashy novel, pretending, as all children do, that she was not with her parents.

It was left to a lone, and hopefully athletic, child to run the mile and a bit from the scene of the incident and raise the alarm. Precious time was lost as the child related the unfolding incident to his parents only to be met with disbelief. It was like the time he had insisted the milk float was on fire his parents commented, or when he broke the window in the greenhouse and claimed a large bird, possibly from foreign parts and carrying nesting materials had done it. Soon a second harbinger arrived breathless, and the air of indifference along the beach was galvanised into panic.

By now the sharp eyes of the Coastguard and the Royal Lifeboat had been alerted and our doomed hero might just have made out, on the receding horizon, the sight of large rockets being fired at one end of the beach, followed several seconds later by the sonic boom of their explosion as the lifeboat crew were summoned. As his teeth chattered and he pondered his fate, he might also have cursed his luck on missing out on the firework display.

To get the lifeboat to the sea at such a time involved towing it with a substantial amphibious tractor across the undulating sand. This could take another fifteen to twenty minutes, perhaps longer if the holidaymakers who had commandeered the prime location of the wooden launching ramp refuse to vacate their deckchair positions. "Hang on mate, if this is an emergency ramp there should be a sign saying so!"

The lifeboat man, showing greater patience than the situation demanded would remove the holiday maker's jacket from the sign which read 'Ple Cle Ti' to reveal the full message… 'Please Keep Clear At All Times'.

"Fair enough!" would respond the argumentative holidaymaker and grudgingly remove their deckchairs. In such ways precious minutes were wasted because people determinedly on holiday were not prepared to let anything get in the way of their enjoyment – and certainly not an obese boy from Birmingham on a tractor tyre receding into the Irish Sea.

Meanwhile, our obese boy, five miles out, was losing hope and consciousness simultaneously. As the spectacle of the launch of the lifeboat proceeded, as much appreciated by the holidaymakers as any other part of the holiday entertainment, our family nibbled on their sandy egg sandwiches and the wife casually asked her husband, "Where's our Lee? Not like him to miss egg sandwiches!"

Chapter Ten
PUNCH

I can't really say how this one got started but start it did.

She was the niece of my Auntie Mary. Although she wasn't my auntie really, she was the oldest of my mum's friends, they had been through primary and secondary school together, even the war together. According to my Mum they had even been walking together back from a concert at the American camp in the war, when the ghost nun had walked through them – but that's another story.

Anyway, because of all this Andrea was actually, though not technically, my cousin, as were loads of other people I half knew in the town. She was average height with short blond hair and a permanent sullen look. She lived over the other side of town – the part whose streets were a mystery to me - so I did not see her on a regular basis. We tended to see each other at Christmas or Easter Time when all the families did their pilgrimage delivering Easter Eggs or Christmas presents. I vaguely remember making mud pies in the garden with her in the dim past, but other than that I think our only communication must have been pulling faces at each other whenever our parents met.

I knew I had no feelings about her either way – which in itself was unusual as I tended to either like or dislike people reasonably intensely at that age. Had I been familiar with the word at the time, which I certainly was not, I'd probably say that I was indifferent to her – she made very little impression on me at all. Things had not changed by the time we had got to primary school. She was slightly taller and much more blonde now but still nothing.

The day in question, which was in the last year of our time at the primary school, I was on door duty, which was a dirty job picked up from the teachers. This strange set of circumstances came about because we had inherited the job of prefect with the bright green badge to go with it. The reason we had inherited this job at the age of ten when this was usually reserved for eleven year olds was because the eleven year olds were busy taking the mystical 11 plus examination which would decide their fates and their life chances. The 'lucky' individuals in the year below found themselves appointed prefects and given supervisory duties around school. These tended to involve barring doors to every pupil at break and lunchtime and then standing behind them listening to the taunts of their erstwhile mates.

Anyway, to return to Andrea, on the day in question I must have said, "Hello" or something equally inflammatory to her as, half way through lunchtime, the door we were guarding was pounded by a large and clearly angry fist – distinctly different from the knock and run tactics of the smaller annoyances.

"Hughes, get out here, I'm going to kick your head in!"

I did not recognise the voice at first but the tone certainly suggested this was not an idle threat. The invitation to open the door, walk outside, take a beating and then be rushed bleeding to casualty was very tempting, but I thought it best to decline with silence. Which would have been a fair tactic – he might even have given up in the belief that I was not even there. He might have, but for the fact that my mates from the duty team were now at the window making rude gestures on my behalf and stating that I would be out to knock him out in thirty seconds if he did not clear off.

I couldn't believe my mates would do that – then again I suppose I could. In fact that is exactly what I would have done. Work it through: the prospect of a fight in which you are not directly involved, ringside seats and the potential to explore intimately the question: 'what exactly does brain matter look like?'

By now, circumstances were escalating. I was running through my options and was clinging desperately to the one where this was a put up job by one of my mates, when Glyn, always the slowest of the group, all the other baying voices having subsided, delivered his considered statement.

"Yeah, Robbins, he's going to snap your legs!"

It was a lame statement, as menacing as blancmange, and I was embarrassed for him for making it. But Glyn had an air of self-satisfaction about him which comes from being the person who thinks he has had the last word.

The true seriousness of the situation now dawned on me. It was Robbins. This was bad. This was very bad. Robbins had not been in my class so he was an unknown quantity. In your own class you have six years to fight, play fight, squabble and generally establish a pecking order as to who is the hardest. The process is much the same as the elephant seals and wildebeest you see on the wildlife programmes battering the hell out of each other to establish dominance in the herd. The secret of being successful is to challenge only those below you in the pecking order and avoid, or make alliances with, those above you – in this way civilisation is maintained in the playground and the Serengeti.

The problem was I did not know where Robbins featured in the pecking order as he had been in the B class and I did not know the violence exchange rate between the two classes. On the surface, things did not look good. Robbins had a huge, bulbous neck and was built like a large, brick lavatory block. I was particularly reminded of this as I stared through the keyhole to size him up. The toilet block which should have appeared behind him had been eclipsed by the square bulk of his frame. I doubted that he would be up to taking on Woody who was our undisputed champion of violence. Then again, no-one in their right mind took on Woody, not even teachers, so this was little consolation.

"Get this door open, Hughes! You've been talking to my girlfriend Andrea!"

A glimmer of hope. At least I understood his motivation now. He obviously didn't understand that she was my cousin (who wasn't) and therefore anything I said to her was more family talk than anything else and…at this point my reasoning tailed off. Too subtle for Robbins, too subtle by half. I wasn't going to be able to talk him down from this one.

Anyway, I was behind a locked door so what was I worrying about? Plenty, actually. On the one hand the bell was five minutes away at which point my mates would be happily opening the door, winding up Robbins further, if that was possible, and pointing him very specifically in my direction. On the other hand, there was a fair chance, on current showing, that the door would not survive for five minutes, given the battering that Robbins was currently inflicting on it.

I briefly considered the melt down option – leg it and hide until the end of the school day - and decided that it was both impractical and would seriously damage my credibility.

It ended up at the Sherlock Holmes thing, "When you have exhausted all the possibilities – what is left, however improbable, is the solution."

It was incredibly improbable, what I did next. I think it was interpreted as the bravest thing I did in school – although the decision was arrived at by elimination rather than any element of courage – bravery was for fools – this was desperation.

I unlocked the door and stepped outside. My fellow prefects gasped at my composure, from which I gathered that they could not hear the alarm bells going off in my head. Even Robbins was taken aback briefly – he stepped back, conceding ground. I hoped I had given him pause for thought. To have brazenly stepped out like this must mean that I thought I could take him. I hoped this was what he was reasoning. Unfortunately, the alternative reason was simply that he wanted a better run up to deliver the killer, brain-opening blow. On reflection, I think he was taking the latter option.

Having said that, he did seem to hesitate slightly. This was not what he had come to expect from potential victims. His gang propelled him forward to within striking distance and my prefect gang offered moral support and verbal encouragement from the now locked door. This, I felt, was very big of them.

I noticed, among the rapidly assembled hordes that made a series of concentric circles around us, some of my erstwhile friends. They all seemed to flash me the 'of course we are still your friends and will definitely rally round you when Robbins has finished with you – but this is a lifetime opportunity to see brain matter first hand' look. I found this less than encouraging.

Having stared narrow-eyed at each other for what seemed an eternity, I decided to break the impasse. It would be the only opportunity I had to seize the initiative. I drew a sharp intake of breath, desperately tried to unlock my clenched jaw and muttered, "Well?"

As speeches go it was short on charisma, argument, coherence and magic. In its favour, it was concise. I had intended saying more but my mouth had dried up. I hoped he had heard it in deep bass, but I had a horrible feeling it had come out in a quavering tremolo.

Clearly, this unsettled him and he felt the need to respond.

"If I catch you talking to my..." and his words tailed off and the exhortation from the crowd came up:

"Smack him!"

Ever the crowd pleaser, Robbins drew back his ham fist and it described an arc in slow motion towards my jaw. I had time to panic, break nervous wind, wonder what we would have for tea tonight when this horrible incident would thankfully be in the past tense, and wince. Unfortunately, what I did not have time to do was move.

The fist hit me square on the jaw line and seemed to keep on coming, through the skin, the bone, my fillings, my nasal cavity and out the ear on the other side.

My brain felt like a ruler twanged on the desk – vibrating and jangling my thoughts, but I managed to assemble three words from what remained of my vocabulary. The three words were...

"Is that it?"

The words were meant to signify me asking Robbins' permission to withdraw to the safety behind the locked door to staunch the salty blood flow that was filling my mouth and maybe cry a little in private.

How, in fact, he interpreted them was me disdainfully dismissing his best shot and getting ready to land a hay baler of my own. Never one for words, Robbins began hesitantly to try and retrieve what he now saw as a changed situation.

"Yeah...well...let that be a..." and, at that point, to my utter astonishment and infinite relief, he turned and fled with his small cohort of followers and seconds.

I stood rooted to the spot, defiant and magnificent, or rather unable to get my body to take on the instructions – turn round, walk back indoors, try to look cool and try to stop yourself bleeding to death from your mouth.

Three seconds later the body kicked in and I slowly started to move back to the shelter behind the door. That three seconds was all it took for the mood of the crowd to change completely – suddenly I was the hero for standing up to Robbins and they headed off in pursuit of their erstwhile tormentor as hounds pursue a wounded fox. My place in the pecking order had soared immeasurably – which in itself would lead to more difficulties later.

My fellow prefects greeted me with open mouthed admiration as I passed slowly and deliberately through them. There was back slapping and words of encouragement from the two-faced gits. I would have milked the occasion but the volume of blood in my mouth prevented any bragging on my part. I moved steadily to the toilet area where I buried my head in one of the dirty roller towels and screamed the silent bloody scream of the mortally wounded animal.

Somewhere in the dark and vibrating jelly that was my brain a still, calm voice, which sounded uncannily like my mum's said, "Don't you ever do anything so stupid again!" and I vowed, absolutely and definitely, not to.

Chapter Eleven
PRESENT

Once Bonfire Night was out of the way, thoughts, most naturally, turned to Christmas.

There were so many rituals in the countdown to Christmas that made the anticipation of the event almost too much to bear. Most of the rituals were in the control of the parents: where to hide the presents; when to decorate the tree; how to blow up the balloons. But one ritual always lay with the children and I believe it continues today.

It would begin with a tickling sensation in the back of the throat, an inability to sit still and generally to be very restless and irritating. The thought of Christmas presents would make me both creepy and bold and I would choose my moment to approach mum.

"Muuuuum," I would begin in a voice so treacly you could make a sponge pudding out of it.

"Muuuum, if I'm very gooood," the syrup continued, "can I have a ...?" and here was placed the latest fad of the season, or one of the old standbys – the bike, the train set, the dog, the thing that the lad next door had, the thing the lad next door was going to have. Actually, there was no lad next door. At this time it was sullen, moping Daphne, and I knew what she was getting for Christmas as her mum had shouted out of the kitchen one day "Daphne Walton, if you don't pull your socks up you'll be getting two slapped legs for Christmas."

It didn't seem like much of a present to me but they were from Birmingham and perhaps traditions were different there.

For my family, Christmas was always a strain. There was always an imbalance between what we desired and what my parents could afford. There could be no new bicycle in our household and you wondered what would be bought that would measure up in our eyes to less than one brand, gleaming, new bicycle.

Of course, we could use the moral blackmail card...

"Fair enough Mum, I'll manage to walk or run to keep up with all my friends who will have a new bike. Don't let it worry you though, I don't want to make a fuss. I'll no doubt get used to the idea of being the only one without a new bike in the whole estate. Just think, running to keep up with all my friends will make me super fit. When I win an Olympic Gold for long-distance running, I'll be able to put it down to you and your refusal to buy me a bike – not buying me a bike will probably make you a hero in future! So I'm sure we'll all have cause to be grateful for the fact that you refused to buy me a new bike in future. I'm going to my room now to work out what to say to my friends when they come round to ask me if I'd like to go out with them on a bike ride after Christmas. But don't let that bother you, I probably won't be damaged in the long run – it is only now that it really hurts."

And I'd flounce out of the room and peep through the crack in the door to see the effect of my handiwork on my mum's emotions. The answer was nothing – she had switched off from my first sentence.

In truth, most of my friends would not be getting new bikes themselves, but some would, and they were enough to justify their inclusion in my plea.

Most of my friends came from the same Reso estate as me, and most parents had the same financial embarrassment at Christmas. Unlike my parents though, some thought little about going into debt for the year to finance the Christmas spend up. Such a thought would never have occurred to my parents, who worked hard and attempted to save hard, but never quite got ahead of the game. There was always that extra unexpected bill or expense to pull them back.

This year I must have been doubly persistent as eventually my mother took me to one side and, in the manner of Jesus, proceeded with the following parable by way of explanation of the true meaning of Christmas:

"There was once a family, much like my own who lived in Stoke on Trent in the Potteries." Now I'd never been to Stoke on Trent but it conjured up an image of factories, smoke and Coronation Street back-to-back houses. Drab people eking out a living in terrible conditions – people, in short, much like ourselves but much worse off.

The particular family that my mother described consisted of a Mummy, who was in her early thirties, but looked, from the cares she wore on her face, much older. There were three lively children: Susan who was ten, John who was eight and Sarah who was seven. The family was tragically incomplete as there was no daddy, for daddy had been killed at work when he had entered the kilns, which were the trademark of the local pottery industry, and one of them had collapsed on him, killing him instantly.

She'd stopped here to let me take in the scene and ask any questions about the character of this family.

The family were facing their first Christmas together without Daddy and a bleak one beckoned. For without Daddy's wages, the family was struggling; there were no extra treats, no weekend sweets and no outings. This year it looked as though there would be few presents either, as Mummy struggled to make meagre ends meet.

Despite this, as with me, the middle of November had brought the familiar high pitched, whining pleading for new toys in exchange for promises of pre-Christmas goodness. All this fell on stony ears as the mother could hardly bear to think about a Christmas, let alone plan for it without any money.

Susan, the eldest of the children at the ripe age of ten, could understand this, and the crying that came from downstairs when mummy had finally put all the children to bed. But what could a little ten year old girl do about it?

My mother looked directly at me, inviting me to put myself in the position of the Mum in the story.

The first week of December in the 1960s, was always marked on television by the construction of the Blue Peter Christmas Advent Calendar from a selection of old coat hangers and some Christmas tree decoration. Blue Peter presenters in those days always came in packs of three. There was the stern and sensible older sister character, the smug boring one with the dodgy taste in jumpers and the jovial incompetent one who always ended up with the job of constructing the latest transformation of useless household items into useless gifts, artwork or jewellery.

And so it came to pass that, at the very end of the programme, the sensible girl stated, "On Thursday's programme, John will be showing you how to make a companion writing set for a really unusual Christmas gift for your friends or family!"

Unusual indeed, and probably unwanted, unnecessary and unappreciated – but for Susan, in her tender years, this project spelled possible Christmas salvation for the family.

That Thursday, Susan perched herself in front of the television, having surrounded herself with the staple requirements of any such challenging construction. She had correctly guessed that this project would entail the assembly of some sticky-back plastic, a breakfast cereal packet and a washing up liquid container. She had scavenged around the house for these items and had included some milk bottle tops, some corrugated card and a compass for good measure.

After some shenanigans involving the naming of the latest Blue Peter pet and a piece on a man who planned to ride a unicycle from Land's End to John O'Groats whilst whistling tunes from the great musicals, John duly appeared to deliver the 'show and make' slot.

John earnestly went through the exotic list of ingredients and made a particular point of stressing the potential dangers of the sharp scissors he wielded so inexpertly as to stab his palm and draw blood during the homily. He winced painfully, and had this been colour television the viewers would have been treated to a trickle of blood emerging from his right palm as he attempted to cut and paste the measured pieces of card and plastic into a semblance of a structure.

Perhaps it was the blood, but the components would not fit or fix together. The sticky backed plastic did live up to its name, showing an alarming propensity to stick to everything, the desk, John's fingers, John's forehead, but not, it would appear, to the construction. At the point that all dignity was lost and the model was irretrievably reduced to the best constructed piece of rubbish ever manufactured by human hands, John reached below the desk and produced a perfect representation of the planned model with the time honoured phrase, "and here's one I made earlier!"

The little liar. For this model was made by someone who knew what they were doing, had command of their faculties and some manual dexterity, unlike John, who was now in some state of near collapse induced by a combination of the hot studio lights and the loss of blood from the gaping hand wound.

This model was carefully finished in a tasteful spotted plastic, and comprised a tube in which to place pens and pencils, a small drawer for paper and envelopes and a space for resting your paper whilst writing.

As John signed off his piece and collapsed in a heap behind his work desk, it was left to Val to light the second Advent Calendar candle. Cue Christmas music, cue end credits, cue first-aider.

My mum and I recounted to each other the time when a rampant baby elephant had pooed and urinated in the studio and John had slipped in it – typical John! And then we were back to the story...

Susan knew what she had to do and set about it with gusto. Between the Thursday evening and the Monday morning she was able to manufacture six of these "presents". For this commercial production line was designed to provide the family with the necessary funds to enjoy a bumper Christmas treat.

That Susan did not have a worldly grasp of the economics of production was hardly her fault. She boldly set foot in the primary playground that crisp Monday morning with the full expectation that she would sell each of the "presents" for a handsome profit which she would place in the hands of a delighted mother who would proceed to smile and arrange a "bumper" Christmas.

In the time honoured manner of primary school children looking to initiate a game, or gather a crowd, she paraded around the playground with that strange mincing gait that only young children can master successfully. She topped this off with a banshee chant of "Who wants to buy... some lovely Christmas presents... just for your friends?"

Others joined in and like some pied piper of garbage she had soon gathered a small crowd.

She produced the six "companion writing sets" from behind the mobile and launched into her prepared spiel, "Who would like to buy a beautiful companion writing set (as seen on Blue Peter) as a present for your friends or family. All the money from the sale of these presents will be going to my mum for her to cheer up and give us a nice Christmas," she proclaimed in the manner of an Oxfam charity advert.

The crowd was animated, but unimpressed, and it was left for Linda, Susan's best friend to start the bidding. Knowing the desperate circumstances that had prompted Susan's entry into the seasonal gift market, she loudly and ceremoniously opened the buying, handing over her week's dinner money for the first of the companion sets. She hoped her largesse would prompt others, and, feeling that they might be missing out on something, some of the girls began to turn over their own dinner money in their sweaty palms with a view to a purchase. In such ways females develop the appetite for the bargain.

Further transactions were postponed by the arrival of Veronica, the playground terror with the two weak-willed limpets who always accompanied her and hung on her every threat.

"What's going on here?" she enquired in her monotone deep voice.

"I have made some Christmas gifts (as seen on Blue Peter) for my friends and when I have sold them all I am going to give all the money to my mum so that we can have a nice, or bumper, Christmas," declared Susan with a trembling voice.

"Christmas gifts – I don't see no Christmas gifts, do you girls?" at which her cronies hissed in agreement, "Just a pile of rubbish stuck together with sticky-backed plastic."

"Don't say that Veronica, please don't say that…" but the rest of Susan's words were drowned out in a rising crescendo of noisy expectation among the assembled host.

"I feel a rumble coming on, do you girls?" declared the towering Veronica.

"No!" said Susan, "Please don't rumble all over my companion writing sets (as seen on…)…"

But the rest was lost in a trademark Veronica bludgeoning attack on the presents and within seconds the multitude of anxious shoppers had become a frenzy of flying fists, biting teeth and hollering savages all enveloped in a flurry of dismembered companion writing sets (as seen on Blue Peter).

The tornado lasted no more than a few seconds and was promptly interrupted by the teacher ringing the hand-bell which signified the end of play time. As one, the maelstrom of girls moved towards the classroom leaving poor Susan in a snowstorm of sticky backed plastic which, where it stuck to her hair, looked like acute polka-dotted dandruff.

The playground was now empty and silent. Save for Susan, distraught, mouth open and eyes squeezed shut.

My mum paused again as we drank in the scene in the playground.

Mrs Flanagan, the kindly teacher, with her trademark sensible plain shoes, floral print dress and anorak, made her way to the lone figure.

"Susan Dear, whatever is the matter?" she exclaimed to the bedraggled spectacle.

But Susan did not reply. Her body was building up to the critical mass needed to induce a major crying fit. It seemed that she was dragging her emotions up from her socks, her chest pulsated, her arms shook, her legs drained of blood.

It sounded not unlike an early morning car with choke or starter problems, a series of punctuated sobs which grew ever more insistent.

"Come on Susan," said the kindly teacher in a phrase she would come to regret, "spit it out."

Unfortunate choice of words. Susan drew in an enormous breath and with an ear piercing half-roar, half-cry that could be heard a mile away, she wailed.

Lamentably, she made the mistake of trying to explain her troubles at the same time as bawling her eyes out. This had two unfortunate side effects. What Susan was trying to say was, "I'd made these companion writing sets (as seen on Blue Peter) and was trying to sell them to my friends when Veronica came over and disturbed my enterprise. I would truly like to kill her as I was gathering funds for my family for Christmas!"

What registered with Mrs Flanagan was: "WWHHAAAAAHH Blue Peter WHHHHAAAAAAA Veronica WWWHHHAAAHH kill her WWWWWHHHAAAAAHHHH for Christmas."

Which seemed a little cryptic for Mrs Flanagan – perhaps Susan had confused the religious significance of Christmas for Easter, but how Veronica could be confused for the crucified Christ escaped her. It was while she was untangling this conundrum that the second side-effect manifested itself in the form of the outpouring of liquids from every orifice of Susan's face.

Her eyes produced copious amounts of tears, her mouth was a dribbling smudge. A little more emotion would have made her ears bleed. But most disturbing of all was the trail of almost fluorescent, thick mucous which emanated from her nose and was of such a glutinous consistency that it moved rhythmically in the space between her upper lip and her nose like some camouflaged slug.

"Come with me dear and we'll tidy you up," was all that Mrs Flanagan could manage by way of reply.

That night as the wind howled, the rain beat on the roof of the tiny two up, two down terraced house, Mummy sat downstairs in the darkened living room sobbing and Susan lay, face down, blubbing quietly into her damp pillow and thinking of better times, and the humiliation of the playground.

My mum had painted such a vivid picture that I could feel my eyes prickling now.

It is often said, by those who have spent a considerable time on this planet, that the darkest hour is that before the dawn.

Susan slept fitfully that night. Her mind wandered to happier times, of past Christmases, of birthdays and Bonfire Nights. In the middle of the night she became so agitated in her sleep that she parted company with her eiderdown and most of her sheets and woke with a start an hour later, freezing cold. As she lapsed back into sleep, she dreamt one of those vivid dreams, the kind you can pause and replay in your sleeping mind's eye. And in this dream she found a solution. So when she awoke the next morning the pain and tears of the night before had been put far behind her.

The solution was obvious and simple. She would make a direct appeal to the person that would not let her down – she would appeal to Father Christmas himself.

She bolted her breakfast of toast and made as an excuse the need to retire to her room to complete some homework.

Once there, she set on the antique writing desk of dark mahogany which her Gran had left her in her will, her best pen and the two sheets of best Basildon Bond Premium Writing Paper, which she had filched from her mum's writing drawer in the kitchen. This was going to be a secret assignment and one which required great concentration. She replaced the cartridge in her Platignum pen, plumped up her shoulders and assumed her best writing position.

She placed one sheet of paper under the other to obtain a firm and secure surface and began to write. As Mr Angus Maciver's First Aid in English had taught, she wanted to keep the style formal, but friendly. Mr Maciver's book was the Bible of learning all things about the English Language. Thanks to Mr Maciver, she had learnt about masculine, feminine, common and neuter gender, that the collective noun for Bishops was a bench and that grouse (or was it grices) collected together in coveys, unlike rooks that congregated in a building.

She was wondering whether the rooks knew that, when she realised that she was wasting time.

Mr Maciver would have been pleased with the result of the next hour's intensive work. It was punctuated once or twice with tears, but generally, the spelling and layout were sound.

Dear Father Christmas,

I know you are very busy at the moment, what with all the boys and girls writing to you with their lists of presents, and I know that your pixies and fairies are very busy too, but I hope you have time to read my letter and help me.

My dad died in the summer in his factory and mummy is still very sad. My brother and sister keep going on about presents, but I know mummy hasn't got any money to pay for them. Every night when she thinks we are all asleep she sits downstairs in the dark, crying very quietly. So I thought I would try and cheer her up. I made some companion writing sets (as seen on Blue Peter) which were v. good (She had learnt to use this term as all the teachers used it in her books), *but that cow Veronica and her mates ripped them up* (At this point Susan had come to an abrupt stop as the anger and hurt of yesterday flooded back, and a couple of poignant tears dropped on to the writing paper, making a slight watery smudge on the previous paragraph. She gathered herself and continued.)

So, this year, Father Christmas, I don't want you to send any presents to me, oh no, just send some money to mummy so that she stops worrying and can begin to enjoy herself. It would be great if you could send £25 as we would then have more than enough for a good time. (Susan was clearly in full flow now as her little pointy tongue was darting out of the side of her mouth and making little figures of eight as she wrote.)

So please Father Christmas, don't let us down.

Lots of hugs and kisses to you,   XXXXXXXX
The reindeer   XXXXXXXXXXXXX
And all your elves and fairies   XX
Lots of love from
Susan Hooper
Aged 10 ½
P.S. I know you will help us.

Susan carefully replaced the lid on the pen and did that strange thing that young girls do when they are pleased with their work. She lifted her forearms up to her chin, wiggled her nose and shrugged her shoulders.

Carefully folding the writing paper three times, she slipped it into the envelope purloined from her mum's drawer for the purpose, and took up her pen once more to write the address.

The first part was easy:

Father Christmas,
Reindeer land,
The North Pole.

So far, so good, but what was his postcode? She knew from the big posters around town that letters without a postcode risked arriving late, or not at all. Time was now of the essence and that would never do.

She settled for: *NP1*

For North Pole one - on the basis that if it got that close to the North Pole then one of his neighbours was bound to re-direct it.

She played with the idea of adding:

The World,
The Solar System,
The Universe

But thought better of it as Father Christmas might not appreciate it and might decide not even to read her letter, let alone help her.

Susan minced to the post-box and sent her letter first class, a weight off her mind.

It was now merely a matter of time before Father Christmas replied and a cheque arrived for Mummy. Every morning, Susan was first up to check the post but most were in brown envelopes for Mummy from her friends, Bill. Mummy had a lot of friends called Bill, and they all sent her regular letters, some in red writing demanding her attention. So they must have been quite keen on her.

After a week, Susan was beginning to give up hope as the brown envelopes continued to plop on the mat. She sat on the stairs and watched the trickle of brown plop when, from nowhere, the sun suddenly shone from behind a cloud and cascaded through the stained glass of the door window casting a rainbow across the hall linoleum, and through this rainbow fluttered a crisp, white envelope addressed to Susan.

"Gosh!" said Susan aloud. Gosh indeed.

What had happened to Susan's letter after she had posted it was that it had arrived in a sack at the sorting office and, because it had been incorrectly postcoded, the machine had spewed it out for hand sorting.

The postman had put it in the second sack of the day addressed to Father Christmas. When another postman had come to collect that second sack, it had fallen out, onto the floor and the postman, who had children of his own, had smiled, guessing it to be the work of a girl, as few boys would go to such trouble. He wondered how the list in this letter would compare with the endless desires of his own daughter. And then he did a naughty thing. As the letter had failed to seal properly he opened it to have a quick read. What he read brought tears to his eyes and he put the letter in his pocket and took it with him when he went on his lunch break. This was strictly against the rules.

In the canteen, amongst the busily eating postmen, he banged on the desk with a spoon and asked to speak to them for a few seconds.

"We got a letter this morning."

The postmen were clearly unimpressed for that was in fact the nature of their business.

"Addressed to Father Christmas."

Again this was nothing unusual and hardly warranted interrupting their meal.

"And as it was not properly sealed down I opened it and read it."

There was hushed silence for a moment, and then, "That's a sacking offence that is!" chorused the postmen.

"I know, but I'd like to read the letter to you and see if we can do something to help."

"Dear Father Christmas..." he began.

By the time he had finished reading, there was further hushed silence and not a dry eye in the canteen. Postmen of all ages were reaching into their pockets for all the loose change they could muster.

"Thanks lads," said our hero postie, "I was hoping you'd react like that. I'll turn this change into some crisp notes and send them back to the little girl with a letter from Father Christmas."

And they all trooped out of the canteen having spread some of the real meaning of Christmas. Sometimes it is better to give than to receive.

My mother chose this point to pause again so that this message would not be lost on me, with my excessive whining about bicycles.

So this was the source of the white letter that Susan was presently rushing upstairs to open. She sat on the bed, her heart pounding with excitement and those little pulses banging in her ears.

She opened the letter and four crisp five pound notes drifted onto the eiderdown and lay there with the Queen's face winking at her.

"Gosh!" thought Susan and then she Goshed out loud.

And so Susan and her Mum and family had the Christmas they desired. And there the story would have ended.

But a week after Christmas when all the excitement had died down, the same postman recognised the handwriting on a new letter, same neat script and same address. He had a warm feeling inside as he took the letter up to the canteen and announced that, "The little girl we sent the money to has written back." They all aahhed collectively in an aahhing of postmen. The postie read the letter aloud,

"Dear Father Christmas,

Thank you so much for the money we had the bestest Christmas in the world. When mummy first saw the money she thought I'd nicked it. And when I explained it had come from Father Christmas she hit me. But it was all right when I showed her the letter. I don't think she believed in you before but she does now!

She bought too much food and presents and decorations and a tree with lights. It was great.

So thanks very much Father Christmas,
Lots of love and cuddles from
Susan and her Mum
xxxxx   xxxxxx"

At this point many of the postmen were back blubbing – but then the postman spotted a PS right at the bottom of the letter... and brought it to the attention of the kind-hearted throng

P.S. Dear Father Christmas, I know I asked for twenty five pounds but only twenty pounds came – but don't worry because mummy reckons it must be those thieving gits down the post office what nicked it.

At which point there was a second's silence before my mum and me burst out laughing. I'd forgotten what had started the conversation. I remembered on Boxing Day though – it was a bike and I didn't get one. I was left playing with my plastic soldiers whilst my mates paraded their bikes up and down the estate.

Chapter Twelve
BIKE

Due to favourable world economic trends, or merely good luck on my part, the next year I did get a bicycle for Christmas. It was second hand but my dad had hidden it at my Uncle Will's and had spent several weekends painting it light blue and fettling it.

Granted the gears did not work, but you could see all the mechanism and cogs gleaming and I used to kid on that I had an automatic continental shift system – that also explained why the chain came off regularly – very temperamental these continental systems! It even had an implement on the front fork for carrying a hockey stick or a tennis racket which seemed a little improbable on the Reso estate.

In a world where presents were seldom surprises and usually disappointments, the bike came as a definite surprise. Perhaps that sounds ungrateful on my behalf. Perhaps I was too ambitious in my present demands, but the general feeling at birthdays was one of resignation and disappointment.

The bike was probably the biggest surprise present ever. The work my dad had done to prepare it was even more remarkable given the history of my dad and the bike.

I had played the bike card pretty hard most years. Morning, noon and night it had been, "Can I have a bike Dad?" I'd pestered him before he went to work, when he came home, when he was going to bed before a night shift and when he got up for an afternoon shift. Twice I had got him to breaking point.

The first time he had snapped, "Bike! Bike! I'll give you bike!"

I took that rather literally and thought that it meant that he was going to give me a bike. My mum pointed out that it meant exactly the opposite. This seemed a strange thing to say – but, then again, adults were given to saying strange things.

On the second occasion I'd cornered him in the bathroom as he washed ready for work, stripped down to his vest and with shaving foam on his chin.

"Can I have a bike for my birthday?" I'd asked for the umpteenth time.

He threw down his razor and looked at me like a demented Father Christmas and shouted, *"You mention that bloody bike one more time and I'll knock you into your birthday!"*

I pondered this for a second and came to the conclusion that this would not be a bad deal. It was May at present and my birthday was in October – I could skip five months in the time it took my dad to knock me senseless and for me to regain consciousness, and the bike would be waiting for me.

I was just about to sign up for the deal, indeed my mouth was open and the words were about to flow when my Mum, who had been lurking, managed to whisk me away so I never got to sample my dad's time shifting talents. On reflection, it was probably as well.

So when the bike did arrive, I was surprised and delighted. But deep inside, having to wait so long for it had killed a little of the excitement, as I had resigned myself to being the Indian they called "He who runs without a bike" on the reservation, or to my best friends, "Without a bike".

Despite that, I loved that bike. All in all, the bike was my pride and joy, and whilst I had always been keen to have a go on other people's bikes, I would not let this one out of my sight. Ginger Rodney, whom I never trusted, despite his ability to make milk come out of his nose, was always on at me to have a go on it and I'd always made up some excuse. It's got temperamental continental shift gears. It is made out of lightweight aluminium and I'm not allowed to let anyone else have a go on it. I realised that all my excuses simply deepened his desire to have a go, and the last excuse was really an invitation to nick it.

Part of me would have loved to have seen him try to fence it off to someone with the continental gear story. All in all, it meant that on the main road out of the estate I always had to go like the clappers to avoid being stopped by him.

On two occasions he was lying in wait for me with his air rifle and got me once in the leg and once in the bum. On a third occasion he threw half a house brick at me and it caught me on the ankle but I managed to regain control. My ankle was like a black balloon when I finally limped home but I had maintained the sanctity of my bike.

A theme in these tales has been my anxiety not to get on the wrong side of the law, and unfortunately the bike was to be my undoing here.

Martin Cottam was smaller than me but, fair play, he had always let me have a go on his bike – even his new Chopper. So when he asked for a go on my bike I was in a quandary. Luckily, I had set the seat as high as I possibly could, so that anyone smaller than me could not ride it, so I settled for giving him a crossie instead. Given that the bike now proved difficult to control, I decided to ride on the pavement instead of the road and we set off up the avenue in the direction of town.

After a short time, I was aware of the light revving of a car engine above Martin's incessant chatting. This was not good. Few cars ventured onto the estate and those that spent overnight there might well find themselves bricked up by the next morning. We could play football or cricket on the road for hours without being interrupted by a car. There was only one car that ventured onto the estate with impunity and the fact that this car was keeping pace with me just at the edge of my eye-line did not bode well.

It was all I could do to keep myself steady. Slowly and inevitably the car drew level and I could make out a hideous light blue colour and the bulbous features of a Morris Minor Panda Patrol vehicle. It continued to keep pace with me – taunting me to look round, savouring the agony. I played it like one of those dreams that you can snap out of. But when I bit my lip and tasted the salty thickness of blood in my mouth I knew the dream route would not take me out of this problem.

I then did the IF – it usually worked… IF I can carry on to the next telephone post before he pulls me over, the station will radio him to go to an emergency and I'll get away with it. The next telegraph post came, and went, and still the insistent throb of the car engine.

IF I can get to the post box… but it was no good, my body was beginning to give up the ghost even if my mind were racing. My legs had surrendered and the bike was losing momentum. We were now reduced to the pace of the winning entry in the slow bike race and, with Martin on the cross bar unbalancing me, we were wobbling to an inevitable halt.

The officer leaned across the passenger seat, wound down the window and through gritted teeth simply said, "Stop. Now."

The high-pitched staccato voice, the economy with words, could only mean the worst – Sergeant Walker – the scourge of the estate.

Had it been wartime Sergeant Walker would have been one of the 'shoot first and ask questions later' brigade and he had taken this attitude into his policing duties.

He took great satisfaction in his reputation and didn't miss an opportunity to enhance it by humiliating one of the estate lads. I'm sure that for everyone he scared onto the straight and narrow, he created another who always resented a policeman's uniform. I once saw him take his truncheon to the back of a lad's legs saying, "Sometimes you have to be cruel to be kind sonny. And sometimes, it's just a pleasure."

The lad he hit had simply been playing football when the good sergeant had decided to make a pre-emptive strike. He was one of the better lads on the estate, never in trouble, popular and fair. That night the police made some implacable enemies among lads on the estate, and it was all so unnecessary.

He stopped the car, got out, straightened the creases in his uniform, put on his cap and strode round to where I stood, petrified. He then went through a series of what seemed pointless questions, as he left no space between them for me to form an answer.

What did I think I was doing?

Was I aware of the seriousness with which the law viewed riding on pavements with a road transport vehicle?

Did I realise I could have killed someone with my recklessness?

Six-month imprisonment was the minimum sentence for this offence – did I think it worth it to disobey the law in this frivolous manner?

I settled for no on all counts and tears welled up in my eyes.

"I know your Dad, laddie! Tell him he'd better pack a suitcase for your six-month holiday, pyjamas, toothbrush, that sort of thing – you won't be needing your football things, nor your bike. Plenty of books though, I'm told it gets very lonely at night in those cells. Do I make myself clear, laddie?"

"Yes sergeant." I replied as politely as I could, given my emotional condition, the tears in my eyes, the lump in my throat and the Sahara in my mouth.

"If I ever catch you again riding on the pavement in such a reckless manner, you are going inside. Clear?"

"Yes sergeant sir," was my meek and contrite reply.

With that he stiffened his neck and moved deliberately back to the car, driving off equally slowly and deliberately. We watched him turn off the estate and I collapsed in a heap. I had, on previous experience, no doubt whatsoever that the sergeant was able to carry out this threat and worse.

To my amazement, Martin Cottam collapsed laughing.

"Come on then, let me get back on then."

I thought he must be joking if he thought I was going to give up six months of my life to give him a crossie.

"You don't want to pay any attention to him – he just likes to act big to frighten you."

I was afraid he had succeeded in that.

Martin, seeing the state of disarray I was in, tried a different tack.

"Look," he continued, "he has gone off the estate –probably to go to the police station to clock off – what are the chances of there being another police car on the estate?"

There was a certain logic to this – and even if a different police car stopped me I could claim a first offence given that I was Bulgarian or Spanish and didn't know the rules. On the balance of probabilities, this was the least likely time that Sergeant Walker would see me. Then Martin added the final piece to his argument.

"You're not chicken are you?"

Within seconds, Martin was back up on the crossbar and we were again on our way down the path. Such was the power of the word 'Chicken' on the estate. I rode on with a sudden bravado, taking turns with Martin to say what we'd do to Sergeant Walker if we ever caught him down a dark alley late at night. We took turns to brag assault him with a knee in the goolies, a dead leg, an ear flicking with an elasie band and a pinch on that soft skin on the inside of the arm. We'd have him begging for forgiveness for the way he had treated us. I felt my spirits rise again.

We had not gone more than twenty yards when the chattering of a car engine sounded over my right shoulder. I immediately came to a halt. The passenger window was wound down and from the driver seat, the driver, one Sergeant Walker, who had made three left turns and gone two miles out of his way to arrive behind me, bellowed, "I'll be around to pick you up at six o'clock at the end of my shift. Make sure your Mum has packed the suitcase – one toothbrush and lots of books. Say your goodbyes early – I hate all those tears and screaming. I know where you live!"

With that he sped off.

We had underestimated the deviousness of Sergeant Walker and his mean spiritedness in being prepared to be so petty to get one over on two lads. I dumped Martin Cottam on the pavement and sped home, put the bike under lock and key in the shed and went up to my bedroom complaining of a headache and sore throat.

There I stayed, worried sheet white for two and a half days. That weekend, I painted my bike orange and gave Martin a good slapping.

Chapter Thirteen
MINERS

Despite the fact that the South Wales branch of my mum's family was steeped in the mining tradition, I knew no miners myself. The nearest colliery to us was ten miles up the coast at Point of Ayr. So the closest I got to the bitter tang of coal dust was the wet mustiness of the coal wagons on a damp day as they rolled into the sidings at Rhyl station, and of course, our coal bunker next to the shed where the coal merchant's navvies manhandled the hundredweight sacks off their jerkined shoulders and onto the dusty concrete floor of the bunker.

I should have known miners though, as in the summer months a constant stream of thick accented and blue scarred dads accompanied their families off the trains from the Midlands, from Derby and Nottingham in particular.

Many injured Derbyshire miners sallied forth on crutches or in wheelchairs from the red-bricked edifice that was the Derbyshire Miners Convalescent Home on the promenade. The home was a very large building, in quite an ornate style. It made me wonder what sort of job was mining if it could manage to incapacitate at least fifty miners at a time in just one county. I quickly decided that mining was definitely something I did not want to do.

It was very disconcerting that as my tenth birthday arrived, my only thoughts about what sort of job I might want when I left school, which could be five short years ahead, had fixed on the jobs I knew I did not want to do.

Train Driver still seemed the most appealing, but I knew the days of steam were numbered and I had no desire to drive the motorised boxes which were the diesels.

It was always in the summer, when the sun was at its brightest and the wind in the right direction, that I'd hear the laughter and merriment of the Derbyshire Miners Camp which edged on to the Reso about half a mile from my house. This camp was like a mini-Butlins, built exclusively for the use of miners from Derbyshire as a cheap and cheerful holiday destination.

I could hear announcements on a high-pitched tannoy telling of wondrous activities, of swimming and magic shows, of free ice cream for the 'kiddies' and I always got the same feeling that I was in the wrong place and missing out on things. This same feeling had taken me one Boxing Day to pick up my Uncle Ivor from the church where he was curate. So intent was I not to miss a car ride, I managed to miss the highlight of the year, the family gathering at our house. I, on the return journey, elongated by snow, was being car sick and wishing I were somewhere else.

In spite of this, kids enjoying themselves in the Miner's Camp, without me, was an image which haunted me every summer. In the shadows of the garages behind the parade of shops, where few ventured, you were only a concrete wall away from the action in the camp. But the wall was tall and topped with barbed wire and shards of glass.

On Marsh Road you could wander past the front entrance with its waist-high, brick wall, topped with an iron fence, but this was backed with gaudily painted wood which completely obscured any view inside this cornucopia of delights.

A couple of my friends had parents who worked in the camp as cleaners or maintenance men in the summer months and they regaled me with tales of passes which entitled the holder to free admittance to all shows, unlimited use of the swimming pool and free food in the canteen. Unfortunately these friends were not close enough that I could press my case for one of these golden tickets and I was left trying to inveigle a ticket from them with no more than my puppy eyes.

After all, I wasn't desperate for a ticket, hell no! In fact, I was *really* desperate for a ticket, desperate to distraction! And the more desperate I became, the surer I knew I'd never be sharing the fun that was going on behind those walls.

I contented myself with rubbishing the whole idea of the Miner's Camp. In some ways this was not difficult to do. Every Sunday in the summer holidays, at eleven in the morning, a very peculiar procession emerged from the Miner's Camp, to the insistent beat of a bass drum echoing a brisk pace of left, left, left, right, left. The drum was beaten to within an inch of its life by a sweaty, balding man with small, round, national health glasses. His first few steps, carrying the burden of the drum like some asymmetrical pregnancy, had drenched his underarms with sweat and his greying white uniform shirt showed signs of fraying. He seemed an improbable pied drummer of Derbyshire but, to his rhythm, a corps of white shirted, black-trousered youths with belts and badges, raised bugles and kazoos to their dry lips and began a rendition of Colonel Bogey.

I knew some of these characters vaguely from school, and I stared in disbelief at their tragic appearance. Without any words passing my lips, my look must have conveyed utter disbelief at the way they were demeaning themselves. They stared resolutely dead ahead, only their eyes darted from side to side to assess the damage they were doing to their reputation by taking part in this poor attempt at a farce.

I thought they might be appearing as part of some police or court order. Caught shoplifting and made, as in medieval times, to parade around the town for public humiliation. But these were the dorky kids. The ones who would grass you up, or who sat sullenly in class, not engaging with anyone. These kids had never been invited on a shoplifting spree at Woolies.

Could they really be taking part in this shambles of their own free will? The kazoo, for Heaven's sake! I knew from my own lack of musical talent that the triangle was the most demeaning of instruments, fit only for the musical dunce. I'd had it proffered to me often enough in Music lessons when all the more sexy instruments had been handed out to those without undiagnosed tone deafness. But the kazoo, that was a whole different order of instrument. The kazoo was a remedial instrument.

"You at the back with your eyes too close together – you can whistle the tune."

"But I can't whistle sir!"

"Very well, here's a kazoo."

These were not even the extemporised comb and paper kazoos with which we sometimes amused ourselves when time was passing exceedingly slowly. These were polished metal kazoos, made to look like some natty silver bugle – but they were kazoos all the same. You could imagine the time they had all spent mastering the instrument, and polishing it. How to Master Playing the Kazoo must have been the shortest tome in musical history, a one page document the size of a small Commonwealth stamp! 1. Place kazoo to lips. 2. Hum the tune of your choice. 3. You have now mastered the Kazoo.

The shocking awfulness of the spectacle had me transfixed and I failed to notice the proceeding noise which sounded like litter being rattled almost rhythmically.

To my left, in less than perfect time, emerged from the camp what was the first of a whole regiment of monstrous girls. At their head was a tall, pale, ghost-like girl with lank, waxen hair and a sickly pallor. Her stick thin arms grasped a tambourine which she struck and rattled with all the gusto of a consumptive. Two paces behind her was a plump girl of no more than five, wearing a faded lemon sash proclaiming First Rhyl Morris Troop Mascot.

Whereas the leader and the rest of the troop endeavoured to keep to a straight line, probably on the reasoning that the shortest distance between two points was a straight line, and the sooner they got where they were going, the sooner this ordeal would be over, the young mascot seemed to be lacking in any sense of direction or purpose. She kept veering to the side of the road where a woman in too tight a blouse and too short a skirt attempted to cajole and coerce the youngster to remain at her station. The swelling of this woman's chest might have been mother's pride. Although, on reflection, it could have been something else.

Why do parents have such an interest in humiliating their children? I could only suppose that it was a kind of 'tough love' regime – humiliated today but resilient enough to handle anything the world throws at you tomorrow!

The serried ranks that followed this double act wore short black skirts and velvet waistcoats festooned with campaign medals and ribbons. They all wore white knee length socks and the cheapest of offensive black plimsolls. They were marching in a most peculiar way, bending their knees and raising their thighs to a position perpendicular to their torsos and then slamming them down on the freshly tarred asphalt. This might have had some appeal, in the same way that watching Nazi's goose-stepping could be described as both repellent and fascinating, but the fact that the first battalion of this regiment was made up alternately of consumptive and obese girls made it simply grotesque.

The consumptives looked like highly-strung poodles and the plump girls like circus elephants. Completing this vision of awfulness were the puff balls of what looked like last Christmas' crepe paper which they carried and shook in time to Miss Nosferatu's tambourine instruction.

I felt appalled and deflated as the rising tide of my desire for the opposite sex, which I'd noted recently, quickly receded to the far horizon, leaving only starfish and sea weed exposed.

But as this vision of feminine nastiness passed by me, a second and third troop emerged, followed by a fourth and a fifth, the waistcoat colours and the mascots changed but the overall impression did not. The townships of Meliden, St Asaph, Prestatyn and Abergele were represented, if the sashes were to be believed.

Someone had had the appallingly bad taste to bus in the ugly children from right along the North Wales coast. I could understand Meliden. It was such a no-where place that even ritual humiliation in a larger town might have an appeal as a Sunday morning activity. But the other towns – whatever had possessed them?

What all these girls had in common was that their legs were whiter than their socks. At the necks of the palest girls, and those with freckles, the first signs of raw sun burn were beginning to appear only minutes into their ghastly, cadaverous parade.

They strutted like battery hens, exposed to the light for the first time. Behind them, and with rich blue and gold flag unfurled, came a dozen St John's Ambulance brigade in black uniforms. I was unsure whether their presence was purely ceremonial, or if they were present to tend to the sun and tarmac pounding induced carnage that was sure to overtake the ensemble shortly.

So appalled had I been by the spectacle, that I had missed valuable time ridiculing the kazoo players and I now ran to the head of the procession to add my impromptu rendition of the unauthorised version of the words to Colonel Bogey which consisted of some musings on the location of a piece of Adolf Hitler's anatomy in the Albert Hall, apparently placed there by none other than his own mother!

The errant kazooists aided me in my headlong rush to the front of the queue by stopping and marking time to the beat of the pasty drum, whilst the more asthmatic players caught their breath from the exertion of the last four hundred yards.

I was amused to find their eyes darting from left to right in consternation as a raiding party of my fellow Apaches gathered. I was pleased to have such backup. I knew I could not compete with the mayhem Ginger Rodney and Ronnie could create, and so it provided me with the excuse that I had not instigated any of the disruption should it turn really nasty.

Ronnie and Ginger Rodney had been playing marbles when the parade had interrupted their game. They'd raced across the Clinic Field to join the fun. Ronnie had selected a couple of his favourite ball bearing sixers which his dad could get for him from the GPO. He juggled them in full sight of the melee of kazooists, daring them to anticipate what he was going to do next.

In all honesty, he was not going to throw his prized ball bearings at them; he was far too attached to them for that. I'd beaten one of his sixers with a threer once and I'd had to play long into the night so that Ronnie had the opportunity to win it back off me. Our game had only been completed when my mum called me in with some urgency past nine o'clock and Ronnie insisted that I conceded the game, so attached was he to his barlies. But they didn't know that.

Ginger Rodney had fewer inhibitions. He reached into his bag and pulled out a fist full of oners – the most expendable of glass marbles with a single colour twist inside. He waited for the parade to move off and carefully rolled a handful of the glassy orbs along the tarmac. They rolled slowly up the camber of the road and down the other side. He ordered me over to the other side of the road to collect the marbles and return them to him. "I know exactly how many there were so you'd better return every one of them, or else!" was the accompanying threat.

The effect of the marbles on the kazooists was to induce panic that this was the first of an ever increasing gauntlet of ordeals they were to face. The bass drummer, charged with the leadership of the parade, was torn between his duty to the parade and his rising desire to break ranks and assault the tormentors.

We watched with some satisfaction as his face reddened and the pace of his heart and his drumming increased. Under his manic drumbeat, the head of the parade was now moving at the pace of the Durham Light Infantry in an effort to exit Reso territory.

Whilst the effect of the marbles caused panic at the Head of the parade, in the massed ranks of the crepe paper wielding marchers it caused mayhem. The thin soles of their pumps, coupled to the exaggerated style of their marching, meant that to stamp down on a marble was to risk quite serious injury.

As the first few victims succumbed, they began to break ranks, running and screaming pell-mell in an explosion of faded colours through the Kazooists and down the road off the estate. The less resolute of the Kazooists joined them, giving a final high-pitched blast of their Kazoos to signal their intention before legging it.

The bass drummer was now signalling a quickstep as he broke into a trot as a means of self protection, but continued to try to restore order with a rhythmic beat. All dignity gone, he now tossed a stream of ugly invective in our direction.

We laughed as the drum beat receded. It felt like the Zulu attack I'd witnessed in the eponymous film, but in reverse. We laughed and gathered our marbles carefully. Which I suppose put us in a far healthier mental state than our victims.

Word of these events spread around the estate and I was proud to be numbered among the perpetrators. We looked forward with some relish to the following Sunday when we could re-enact the scene but this time with the whole tribe present.

Alas, it was not to be, for strategically parked in the middle of the route, as conspicuously as possible, was a white and blue Police Panda car with a certain police sergeant standing, arms folded, next to it, moustache twitching. Although some of the braves were up for a confrontation, I skulked back home, not wishing to have any contact with the sergeant after my recent run-in.

Chapter Fourteen
BISCUIT

The first indication that the life we led on the Reso was not the full picture of how things could be, came when we started to visit Auntie Hebe next door.

Again Auntie Hebe was not a real auntie but one based on proximity – as a neighbour she had honorary auntie status conferred on her as she sometimes looked after us if my mum was engaged on some family business elsewhere.

Considering that only a wall separated her front room from ours, circumstances could not have been more different. Auntie Hebe's family were strict, Welsh, chapel going individuals who took things seriously, never swore or raised their voices.

I only discovered the seriousness of the No Swearing pledge when, in conversation with Auntie Hebe over the garden fence, she asked how the family had enjoyed our Sunday walk down by the river, and I had replied word for word that we had all enjoyed it but that, "Auntie Gladys said her feet were bloody killing her."

Auntie Hebe went into a sort of breathing fit in which she pecked at the air with her narrow bird-like features, her eyes expanding behind her large spectacles, before she looked heavenwards and beat a hasty retreat indoors so as not to be further contaminated by this young demon.

I remember thinking that if 'bloody' had that effect on her I could probably induce a coma by introducing her to Sammy Barker.

Charity was one of Auntie Hebe's virtues and the above incident did not prevent her from inviting me into her home when my mum went visiting for morning coffee. Everything about her house was alien and attractive, even coffee.

Tea was the drink of choice for adults in our household. The only coffee in our home was a single, small bottle of Camp coffee, an evil-looking brew which resided from one year's end to the next on the top shelf of the cupboard and looked like, and had the texture of, creosote.

By opening the kitchen drawers, I had once climbed on the fashionable Formica work surface to explore the top cupboard and in particular the Camp coffee with its fancy picture of an Indian soldier on the label. I made the mistake of unscrewing the lid and smelling it. My nose was assaulted by an orchestra of pungent smells, none of which I could imagine drinking from choice. I could understand why such a desperate brew should be placed so high out of harm's reach.

Auntie Hebe had real coffee in a tin, in powder form. Although it smelt no better to me, she turned it into a drink for my mum with complete dexterity. The coffee would always be accompanied by a glass of Corona for me – not the flat stuff that my nain served as an enticement for her grandchildren, and which sat depressed for most of the time between Christmases, but an effervescent concoction which fizzed with flavour in your mouth.

Of course, the drinks would prompt the biscuit barrel to be produced. A biscuit barrel of ample proportions, crafted from a very dark and ancient wood. We did not have a biscuit barrel in our house. We ate biscuits from the packets or from the bags of Woolworth's broken biscuit range. They seldom lasted long enough to be transfered to any other container.

When the lid of the barrel was removed, an array of fancy and expensive biscuits was revealed – biscuits thought of as Christmas specials in our household. Iced biscuits, jam filled biscuits, understated Royal Scot shortcakes and the king of biscuits – the chocolate wholemeal digestive.

We would retire to the front room – the front room no less – for the adults to talk and for me to be seen and not heard. Once, and only once, Auntie Hebe had forgotten the biscuit barrel and I was forced to look long-faced and saucer-eyed at her, like some pathetic puppy dog miming, "Urgently in need of chocolate biscuit to stave off terminal hunger pang."

It was a terrible dilemma in the front room. How to combine politeness with the desire to snaffle as many biscuits as possible. I always worked on the principle with biscuits that you never knew when and where your next chocolate digestive would come from, so you gorged whenever you could. But I didn't want to provoke Auntie Hebe to withdraw my invitation by overstepping the mark, so I took to rearranging the biscuits so that they took up the maximum volume in the barrel and the missing digestives would not be missed.

Chocolate digestives had provoked arguments in my own house as I had implored my mum to buy them on a regular basis. She had replied tersely that she didn't buy chocolate digestives because we'd only eat them. For years I had been satisfied with that answer – and had even quoted it to others. I remember saying to Martin Cottam as I shared his family biscuit stash, "We don't have chocolate biscuits in our house because we would only eat them."

And he asked the question that had so far eluded me, "What else would you do with them?"

I realised I had been conned out of several years worth of digestives by my own mother.

Such were the extreme lengths that my mother went to when hiding biscuits from me that I once found a packet of chocolate fingers hidden in the recesses of the pantry, three years out of date and invested with a grey-white mildew bloom. I wept uncontrollably at the thought of wasted chocolate biscuits and was even tempted to eat them, simply to have the last word.

The two other attractions of a visit to Auntie Hebe's front room were the upright piano and the snow scene.

The former was a well loved piece of family furniture complete with its own candle holders and lace mats on which stood generations of family photographs. The large oak clock which sat on the mantelpiece opposite the piano always seemed to be ticking out "pi-ano pi-ano" slowly and insistently, even when I was thinking of chocolate digestives, and my attention was always drawn to it.

Whilst my mum and Auntie Hebe retreated to the kitchen to make the hot beverages and my Corona, I would dart furtively to the piano and lift the lid. I'd touch the inviting ivory keys as lightly as possible so that they were audible just to me and wander up and down the keyboard repeating those notes which had particular charm.

I don't think Auntie Hebe would have minded me having a play on the piano but I had learnt to my cost that sometimes it was better not to ask. For one thing she might say no and for a second thing my mum would undoubtedly take the view that I had shown her up by asking. My mind was drawn to the second part of the little notices that hung behind the counters of all the shops on the estate,

"Please do not ask for credit. A refusal often offends."

I could never understand how the random notes I played could be put together to form the magnificent hymn music Uncle Herbert could coax out of that piano on a Sunday evening.

By the time they had returned, I would be by the window playing with the large glass snow scene bringing winter to June, which amused me for hours. If challenged about the strangulated musical notes from the piano, I had my story ready: "This Russian looking lad, that I have never seen before, burst in and insisted on playing the piano. I told him that you would not be very happy about it and offered to share the snow scene with him, but he just carried on messing with it. I'm not sure he could understand me, him being Russian or maybe Chilean. Then he dashed off again just before you returned."

In Auntie Hebe's front room, I learnt there were other ways of doing things and of being than the ones I learnt in my house and on the estate. Worlds of music and chocolate biscuits and real instant coffee and it got me thinking.

When you grow up you always think that the way your parents do things is the right way to do it. When you see other people, and especially families, doing things differently you assume that they are wrong. My mum, and therefore I, thought it wrong that Martin's mum went out to work and left the key on the string and that Martin and his brothers and sisters came home to an empty house and had jam sandwiches for tea.

The fact that he loved coming to ours for beans on toast or fish fingers and chips with loads of ketchup simply proved my mum right. But in Auntie Hebe's I saw glimpses of things, well, music and chocolate biscuits mostly, not forgetting the snow scene, which showed that things could be different and also be better.

Chapter Fifteen
SHED

Crossing the end of our garden at 90 degrees was Veronica's garden. It was longer and narrower than ours and Veronica's parents had taken the opportunity to dress it with a variety of crazy paving and coloured stonework flower beds.

As Veronica's dad worked on the council, the crazy paving proved easy to obtain. A council lorry full of the remnants of once perfect paving slabs would arrive and all and sundry could have as much as they could carry.

The coloured stonework seemed more out of keeping. It was clearly not obtained from the council and my parents could never understand why people would make such a permanent investment in a property they would never own. It was only later that I learnt that my dad had an aversion to buying his own property in case something catastrophic happened, like a roof needing replacing. He did not consider that such things might be covered by insurance. His aversion to such risk meant that he left this world owing nothing on a mortgage and with a legacy to me of some garden tools and several bottles of Old Spice after-shave. Not much for a lifetime's hard work.

To the left of our garden was that of the Walton's. They had arrived in the early 1960s from Birmingham with their teenage daughter, Daphne, who had a penchant for floral print shift dresses and beehive hairdos. "Thirteen going on twenty!" was how my mum described Daphne. It was Daphne who had taught me to twist to Chubby Chequer, despite the fact that I had not wanted to learn. The insistent grasp of her porky fingers really left me little option and I made a mental note never to challenge her to an arm wrestling contest. I could imagine her enveloping my fingers in her grasp and applying increasing pressure like a hydraulic jack, biting her lip with determination, her beehive vibrating and humming with exertion.

The Waltons spoke with a nasal whine like gravel lubricated with honey. He was some sort of engineer, never happier than when tinkering with engines of any kind. He'd adjust his glasses and explore the engineering problem to be solved, as if to inject a measure of precision into his working, then step back and hit the offending machinery with a large hammer. His was the original Birmingham screwdriver. He spoke with the same flat tone whether angry, happy or content. This had the serious implication that you never knew if he was joking or deadly serious when he said something to you. I decided that the best course of action was to say as little as possible to Mr Walton and simply smile inanely when I passed him and was greeted with those punctured vowels. He had probably written me off as some kind of simpleton.

Once, when my nain was ill and my mum was called upon to do some nursing, I had to stay at the Walton's for two nights. I found the experience traumatic. The different sights, smells and routines of an alien house, the mental flailing to conform to the way they did things and the incessant and unwelcome interest of both Daphne and Rusty, their wiry, terrier mongrel snapping dog, proved debilitating.

The dog snapped at my heels whenever I sat down, grabbing my trouser legs and shaking its head violently whilst growling in a Birmingham accent. Daphne just watched me. When I looked her way she did not even try to disguise the fact that she was staring at me and it was always me who looked away first in embarrassment. Although I had looked forward to the adventure of a few days in the Walton's house, the reality meant that I was glad to be back in my home, in my own bed, without the nylon sheets, in the wrap around comfort of winceyette.

The downside of this mental and physical torture in the Walton's house was that I looked for something to do with my hands. Mrs Walton, outside her house, was never seen without either one of those tartan pull along shopping trolleys or an oval wicker shopping basket which proved so popular with housewives of the time. The more the dog yapped and Daphne stared, the more I fiddled with my fingers on the shopping basket. The wicker began to give way, slowly at first, but then in large swatches.

Before I had time to gather my thoughts, the damage was not only done, but too soundly done to be repaired. My first thought was to switch the blame onto the dog that was now sleeping soundly, having had the satisfaction of drawing blood from my ankles. Although the dog could not defend himself against the accusation, the timing of this wanton destruction would have pointed the blame back on me.

I decided to slide the remains of the basket under the settee and hope I'd have left in the morning before it was discovered.

Luckily, I was safely back in my house the following morning when through the open kitchen door and along our alleyway the nasal tones of Mrs Walton were heard.

"He's sodding ruined my bloody shopping basket!"

It was not clear whether she meant me or the dog. I decided to say nothing.

All in all I preferred it when the Jones lived there.

Although Mrs Jones kept herself to herself, she let out two bedrooms in the summer to the succession of variety acts which plied their trade for a week in the promenade theatres and then were gone. A succession of acrobats, jugglers and magicians had practised in her back garden and I'd been privy to their acts. They'd shown me tricks, smiled and ruffled my hair. One even made a half-crown appear and disappear before giving it to me saying that I would never be without money as long as I kept that coin. He said it with such earnest sincerity that I determined never to be parted from the half-crown.

I lost it the next day somewhere in the big field playing football and someone else inherited what was meant to be my luck with money. On reflection, they probably converted it to sweets and a Beano so the coin would have remained in circulation until decimal currency came in. No one would know the true value of that coin in their small change, but one day it might make its way back to me.

Then again, how would I recognise that particular coin again? The secret I determined was never to spend any money you obtained. A great theory but not particularly practical.

To the left of our home was a corner house with a narrow tapering garden that came to a point. As well as the chain link fence and concrete posts, this garden had enormous privet hedges some eight feet tall. I don't ever remember anyone being in the garden, either in Auntie Hebe's time or when the Croxteths moved in later.

The fact that the Croxteth garden emitted no noise was more than compensated for by the incessant whine that came through my bedroom wall at night. Every evening, within fifteen minutes of my going to bed, the Croxteth's son, Raymond, would retire to his room to practise the accordion.

The accordion – I ask you! Why would a twenty year old man choose such an instrument? It was neither cool nor practical – a guitar, an organ, or even the drums, I could have understood, but an accordion! My initial reservations were deepened by five years of an hour and a half of Raymond attempting, in a very approximate way, to reproduce the hits of the day whilst I desperately attempted to enter the land of Nod.

It was over this garden that PW and I had used a length of metal washing line post to bazooka bangers at Ronnie, pretending to be a Nazi sentry in his parents' bedroom window.

The bangers made a dull thud as they ignited in the tube and then arced over the hedge to hit Ronnie's window in a splutter of exhausted firework paper. We'd take shelter as the echoing, hollow ring of the firework ricocheted off the walls of buildings and was amplified by the gaps between the houses. Parents would appear, anxious to find the source of the explosion. PW and I would huddle in the rhubarb patch stifling laughter and desperate to breathe. Had the adults looked across, they would have thought some particularly hearty snails were tucking into the rhubarb as the leaves vibrated to our silent laughter. They'd return to their living rooms perplexed and after a suitable and irregular interval, we'd repeat the process.

This was one of my most cherished memories of childhood. It comprised the fun of doing something dangerous and illicit, having PW fund what seemed like an inexhaustible supply of firework ammunition and, best of all, shooting Ronnie/Nazis on a regular basis. It really didn't get any better than that, I remember thinking at the time, and I was dead right.

Where Snowy the rabbit's home-made and substantial hutch met the Roberts' fence, I could lever myself over into Veronica's garden and this I did on a regular basis.

Like the hutch, Veronica was a substantial girl, well made and brooking few arguments. She had oily, olive skin and a good sense of humour for the most part. Being a year older than me, she had the authority of age. Coupled to this was her willingness to lash out indiscriminately at anyone who trespassed against her. So when Veronica said we were playing Queenie-O-Cocoa, Who's Got the Ball? or What's the Time Mr Wolf? that is what we played.

I once infuriated her when we played the skipping game Salt, Pepper, Vinegar, Mustard. I only ever played girly skipping games at Veronica's – I would not be seen dead doing such things in a public place. I'd chosen Mustard which was where the rope whizzed around at amazing speed and you had to jump in and the two people holding the rope would count the revolutions. Inevitably, as the skipper tired they would lose concentration and the rope would whip up and strike them, stingingly, on the ear as they mistimed their jump.

Mustard seldom got into double figures before the unfortunate skipper was given a throbbing ear. On this occasion, Veronica counted to eighty seven before throwing the rope down in exhausted disgust. My victory was short-lived however as, in the act of turning in triumph to the lovely Debbie Parry, who was holding the other end of the rope, Veronica advanced on me and punched me in the ear for showing off. It was not a bright thing to frustrate, irritate or generally cross Veronica.

I detected at times a bubbling resentment towards me, although I could not think what I might have done to warrant this. It might have been the Easter Monday when I squirted Veronica's Sunday best dress from an extended range with puddle water from my dad's bicycle pump. Or perhaps the time I convinced her that Snowy the rabbit's dropping were really currants that my mum used in baking scones. Other than those times, I could think of no reason why she might resent me. But for some reason or other she took a delight in hitting me on a regular and powerful basis.

Despite that, whenever we played house, she always baggsied me, and Ronnie got the delightful blonde, blue eyed and slender Debbie. We would then spend an hour in her shed setting the scene for the game:

"I know, let's pretend you two are footballers and we live in a really big house in a city."

"Yes, and Ronnie plays for United and I play for Liverpool," I'd add.

"No," Veronica would insist, "You both play for United."

"OK, we both play for United and I'm the centre forward and Ronnie is the inside left," I'd insist.

"No. Ronnie is the centre forward and you are the centre half," Veronica would interject.

"Right and I drive a Lotus and Ronnie drives an Aston Martin!" I'd picture.

"No. Ronnie does drive an Aston Martin but you drive a Ford Anglia."

After another five minutes of being shown my place, Ronnie would arrive and Veronica would insist I talked him through his role. He'd be well impressed with his new lifestyle and totally unconcerned that in every facet, luck, or rather Veronica, had not seemed to smile on me at all.

We'd then retire to the garden to play a season's worth of games against imagined opposition whilst the girls continued carefully to construct their imaginary world down to the colour of their bathroom suites, Veronica favouring Avocado, which I always felt was a touch pretentious, whereas Debbie went for Yellow which I thought was both bright and practical.

Half way though an away game at Arsenal, with a disastrous sense of timing, the girls would call us in for our tea and we'd stop our footballing and climb into our cars for the long drive home. Ronnie would career round the garden in his Aston Martin whilst I'd be forced to pootle along in my Ford Anglia.

If I ran in a way that she considered out of character, Veronica would appear at the shed door and remind me that I only had a Ford Anglia. I'd say that I'd put a bigger engine in it and Veronica would state that I had not put a bigger engine in it and that I'd better slow down because I was ruining the game.

Ronnie, out of sight of Veronica, would just laugh and point at me whilst making faces. Debbie would be busy attending to a make believe pan that was make believe overheating on the make believe stove, so I could expect no support from that quarter. I'd quickly pretend to be changing my engine to comply with Veronica's wishes.

"Let's pretend we're having stew and dumplings," I'd say, relishing my favourite meal, "and we've got plenty of brown sauce to put on it."

"It's Friday and we've cooked fish – haddock with white sauce and new potatoes," came the uncompromising reply.

"But I don't like fish – I always get the bones!" I remonstrated. "Ronnie doesn't like fish either."

I looked to Ronnie to back me up but he remained silent and stone faced. He whispered, "It's only a game," to me out of earshot of Veronica.

"I don't like fish. And it isn't Friday, it's Saturday because we've just been playing Arsenal," I continued in vain.

So fish it was. I didn't enjoy the imaginary fish for fear of swallowing an imaginary bone and choking to death in Veronica's shed.

After tea, or dinner as Veronica called it, she started...

"I know, let's pretend that David breaks his leg playing football," and she went on to rehearse Ronnie on how these dreadful events were going to unfold. The prospect of the crunching tackle from behind that threatened to end my professional career really appealed to Ronnie and he outlined, with too much relish for my liking, the kinds of challenges he could make to bring about the fearful injury.

Veronica then made us act out the tackle several times to her satisfaction before the actual event. Ronnie's role play was rather too good as he scythed across the freshly mown lawn into the back of my knee and I really was contorted in pain when the final tackle was delivered.

"Let's pretend that there is bone sticking out and there's blood everywhere and we can't even bear to look." shouted Veronica as I writhed on the ground in rather more than mock pain.

The saving grace of this scenario was that it would hopefully end in my being taken to mock hospital in the shed and being ministered back to health by the delicious Debbie. This was a not too unpleasant eventuality.

Imagine my surprise when I awoke from the mock anaesthetic to find that my surgeon, Ronnie, had reset my leg, Debbie was finishing washing the dishes from the previous meal and that nurse Veronica was busy mummifying me with bandages she had somehow purloined from her sick grandfather and which smelt of the rubbing oil that came in sinister green bottles and whose pungency could strip paint.

Apparently, there had been complications in the operation which explained why my head, arms and both legs were now in the process of being immobilised. I tried to imagine how a leg injury could have developed so grievously. Had they dropped me off the stretcher, or perhaps the ambulance had crashed on the way to hospital?

It suddenly dawned on me, that in the game and in reality, I was now completely restrained and that nurse Veronica was now perched over me eating a family packet of Marks and Spencer salt and vinegar crisps.

I'd always thought that Veronica smelt of salt and vinegar crisps; she certainly ate large quantities of them.

Although my confinement and the slowly diminishing distance between her face and mine was somewhat disturbing, it was also, in some curious way, rather exciting.

Chapter Sixteen
SHIFT

Unlike most people on the Reso I did not know what my dad did at work on a daily basis. Glyn's dad worked for a coal merchant during the week, bagging and weighing the coal from the rusting 16-ton coal wagons in the good's yard adjacent to the station. We could go and see him doing it and it gave us a good official pretext for entering the otherwise prohibited area of the good's yard. I used to love crossing the threshold of the wood and metal gate and entering the grown up world of the railway yard.

Admittedly, it did not look much fun filling one hundredweight coal sacks and manhandling them onto the coal lorries that distributed them to a thousand Rhyl households. Glyn's dad's hands were calloused from the work and his face looked like the miners I'd seen on family visits to South Wales with blue scars where coal dust had entered cuts to give a distinctive tattoo.

I didn't want a job like that but at least I could see how it all worked. You did the work and got paid a wage.

I could also see Glyn's dad in his weekend job as a waiter at the Pavilion theatre on the promenade. He'd collect glasses and deftly deliver drinks from the bar with a large wooden tray. He'd pocket tips and smile grudgingly, as he was not a very affable man. If Glyn's mum accompanied us, we could sit in the sun lounge and he would slip us drinks, bottled lemonade and crisps and at no point did any money change hands. I thought that was pretty good. It was easy to describe what Glyn's dad did for a living.

For my dad it was not so easy. On my birth certificate he was described as a 'shift process worker' and if he had to send off any official documents and my mum asked how he should be described on the form he simply said 'shift process worker' as if this was a very specific and obvious category of work.

I was intrigued by how my dad had become a shift process worker and why. The answer as it turned out, was that it had not been his chosen career path at all but had been forced upon him by the needs of making ends meet for the family. Following the war, when all prospect of a career in management disappeared, my dad came home to find only manual jobs available.

He worked for six years on the railway, on the signal and telegraph gang. He'd once described that job to me and made it sound like a lot of mucking about with some mates in a 'gang', punctuated by a bit of maintenance work. It sounded good to me. Unfortunately, it did not pay well and when an enormous factory was opened by the Courtaulds textile company at Greenfield, some fifteen miles east of Rhyl, my dad applied for and got a job as a shift process worker. Like hundreds of others from Rhyl, he made the daily trek to the factory, initially by bus and later by shared car.

The factory apparently was the largest of its type in the world. It produced Rayon, one of the host of man-made fibres developed by chemists during the war. These were the substitutes for cottons and silks and my dad was part of the transformation process that turned raw chemicals into viscose which was then woven into cloth.

On an infrequent railway journey to Chester, to see a family member who was in hospital there, my dad pointed out the factory. The factory or 'plant' as he called it, straddled the railway and was a mass of wires and pipes and stanchions and chimneys and towers. It was like passing through a metallic digestive system with rusty intestines strewn randomly to left and right and passing over the train at a number of points. Despite moving at some speed, we were still passing through these innards a couple of minutes later, which just went to show the vast scale of the plant.

Steam belched randomly from a number of points and the pipe work was rusted and corroded in a number of places. Where it was painted, this superstructure was in dull browns or a shade of green I'd previously associated with my nain's bread bin – an old green, insipid and sickly.

A number of voluminous chemical storage tanks backed on to the railway and they appeared black, sooty and grimy. My dad pointed out that, on closer inspection, at a certain point this neglect was replaced by a bright silver application of paint. I counted out eight such storage tanks decorated in this manner. My dad explained that the factory had had a royal visit a month previously to receive an award for exports and that one of the managers had carefully walked the route of the royal visitor and decreed that the line of the route be painted so that it would all appear fresh and new – the acceptable face of the chemical industry – for the royal visitor.

Thousands of pounds had been spent on this deception, but had his Royal Highness stepped off the allotted route or deviated from what was planned, the grim reality of where my dad earned his money would become apparent. No wonder, I thought, that the Queen labours under the misapprehension that her world smells of fresh paint.

A wide fan of railway sidings brought in the food to stock the chemical behemoth and took out its precious excrement. These were full of chemical tankers hooked up to intravenous drips feeding the process. I imagined the pipes like so many drinking straws on which this monster sucked furiously.

Pervading the whole site, and drifting on the wind, depending on its direction, was a distinctive and unpalatable odour of bleach and bile. The same odour attached itself to all of my father's work clothes, fading out the colours and making small corroded holes in the cloth where it hissed and splashed on him in the course of a working day.

My dad drove a Coventry Climax fork lift truck at work. I found this difficult to believe. He didn't drive anything whilst at home and was in his forties before he finally learnt to drive, passing on the second attempt. The idea of my dad dodging and weaving in and out of the bunkers and silos, the pipes and crevices of the plant on his fork lift truck did not really add up. But dodge and weave he did.

If ever I asked him what he did at work he talked of bales and viscose and rayon and chemical burns. He made the factory sound like some medieval version of Hell. He spoke of rats, scuttling in and out of the shadows of the tanks and pipes and nesting in the bales of warm rayon. This all seemed so unnatural, especially as what distinguished a Courtaulds' rat was that their legs were worn away to stumps by the constant immersion in puddles of corrosive chemicals on the floors of the baling sheds. Despite this horrible deformity, they chose to stay in the factory with its warmth and the titbits from the workers' snap tins.

I felt that my dad, and all the other dads who worked there, were also prisoners of sorts, as nowhere else along the coast paid as well as Courtaulds for manual labour.

To keep their spirits up, the men would find a raft of ways to fiddle the company of their time or their labour. Despite the fact that they were not supposed to smoke on the site due to the flammable nature of much of the produce, the men took extended toilet breaks where they smoked uninterrupted.

For one random employee, his turn in the toilet cubicle coincided with a surge in the sewage pipe of some badly discharged chemical. He lit up as it belched through the system, exploding and destroying much of the toilet block, and killing its unfortunate occupant. My dad told me this in a matter of fact way, as if it was one of a number of such occurrences, which made it all the more horrific. Perhaps the fact that my dad had spent time in the army in the war meant that he was more accustomed to the scenes of carnage that I had only witnessed secondhand in the pictures of the Vietnam War on television.

I imagined the scene of the incident, and trying to recover parts of the unfortunate man.

Compounding the dire circumstances of this work was the shift system that my dad worked. This seemed to be tantamount to the torture of sleep deprivation. My father, for over thirty years, worked a pattern of mornings, afternoons and night shifts punctuated by three days off in between. The morning shift was between 6 a.m. and 2 p.m. with an hour added on to either end for journey time. By four o'clock he would be home, washed and fed. He'd read the papers and watch the news on television and retire to bed by 10 p.m. This approached normality in his sleep pattern but left him unable to lie in bed beyond 6.a.m. on any day.

He'd be up just after four and would go through his ritual of making a fried breakfast, coughing and wheezing until his lungs got going. I'd sometimes hear the catch on the door engage as he set off with two mates to catch the 4.45 a.m. bus.

Afternoons would be 2 p.m. to 10 p.m. and, although these seemed not unreasonable hours, coming off a set of mornings meant that my father could not sleep the normal pattern and would begin the shift by going to bed at 4 a.m. He'd want silence throughout the morning until he got up at 11 a.m. This could be torture for me, especially in the excitement of school holidays when I'd want to career around the house.

Night shift further disrupted his sleep pattern as the 10 p.m. to 6 a.m. shift meant that in winter he would not see the sun, or even daylight for weeks on end, and in the summer he could not sleep properly for the heat and light. He claimed it would be easier to work permanent nights as then his body could make adjustments on a permanent basis but that was not an option.

It was easier to be out of the house as much as possible given my dad's shift patterns, many of my friends felt the same with their dads going through a similar shift pattern.

I knew I did not want this for my future and was encouraged when either my auntie or my mum said the latest report from school suggested I might be able to avoid this fate. Doing well in school became a preferred option for me because of its promise of a better job than my dad's. I know that many of my mates did not share this view, and I felt as sad for them as they probably felt for me.

Chapter Seventeen
BILIOUS

Planned illness was fine. The sort of illness that bought you time to do other things or which avoided problems, confrontations or exams was highly useful. My planned illnesses tended to be well organised and well staged affairs. I could think myself into symptoms. I did a good shiver, an immaculate, deathly pallor and a formidable sore and husky throat.

I found out that the secret was not to move from rude health to death's door without some carefully laid clues in between. An illness had to be nurtured and carefully developed.

The great planned illnesses had a double bluff in them. This was when my Mum picked up my husky voice and I denied it saying I would be fine. Half an hour later I would become increasingly morose and suggest an early night, claiming a headache and feeling cold. If I sat close enough to the roaring coal fire when they were out of the room and then rapidly moved away when they entered, I could do the feeling cold and the raging temperature bit at the same time. I could also fake the involuntary shivers in the same way that little children, when they are trying their hardest to pinch you, often reach that pitch of effort where their face starts to vibrate and their teeth chatter.

Having an illness vocabulary was useful as well. "I feel sick," was too obvious. No effort, no imagination. I found that the harder you tried to describe the symptoms, the better they sounded. I watched and learnt from my elders and betters. My Auntie Annie, in line with her middle class pretensions, was never sick, she was bilious. It amounted to much the same thing but bilious was so much more descriptive of the internal processes, the swelling of the bile duct, the trembling convulsion of the orifices, and the glorious pebbledash of partly digested food. So much more graphic, and so much more believable.

Nauseous was another good word to use when stumbling around light-headedly. It never failed to induce a quick search for a bucket and flannel in my mum.

The only problem with both these words was that they meant no food.

"It's better not to eat if you are feeling nauseous David, perhaps you might manage a thin arrowroot biscuit tomorrow morning."

My long service medal for being ill was a bottle of Lucozade with a golden-orange see through wrapper on it. Usually this would appear on the third day and I would greet it with mixed feelings. On the one hand, I'd clearly managed a flawless and convincing portrayal of my chosen illness to receive the bottle. On the other hand, I hated Lucozade as it reminded me of the times I had really been ill and, being too ill to resist, was fed it regularly on the hour, every hour, as a pick me up. I'd only ever wanted to put Lucozade down.

It brought back memories of the raging and pulsating ear infection that had driven me to the edge of madness for days on end. It reminded me of a time when I was very young and had crept into my parents' bed and had sweated motionless, too scared to move, as the wolf with the red eyes had circled the room above and below, and appeared at the end of the bed to whisper things to me, rhythmically and loud, which were just out of earshot. That had been the most terrifying time.

Wasting half an hour's television of an evening was more than compensated for by a day off the following morning. Sometimes, I had a plan. It might be to watch some intermittent television, or some school based ordeal, exams or bullies to be avoided, or in deepest winter, to avoid the snow.

I hated the snow. The initial delight of making snowballs and sliding on paths of ice was more than outweighed by the first heavily compacted iceball hitting you in the back of the neck, burning and freezing and working its icy grimness down the nape of your neck.

I had no problem, by the second day of snow, feigning a cold and watching others trudge though the sleet and filthy sludge to school whilst I cosied up to the flannelette sheets.

I'd often time my illness to coincide with the limited television schedule. As the few daytime programmes were interrupted by the test card and some short tourist features of castles in Scotland or historic abbeys in Yorkshire (with stirring orchestral or bagpipe music), there was often little of interest to see.

I've been driven to counting the stripes on the test card before now, or watching that potter turn his clay bowl for what I hoped would be the last time.

Occasionally, there would be schools' television programmes on the box and I'd watch so that I'd not feel guilty about having the day off. My maths did not improve dramatically but I could discuss at length, "the ecological treasures that are the Galapagos Islands," and "the sea swimming iguana that exists there only,". The migration route of the grey whale from its feeding grounds,"off the cold currents of Alaska to its breeding nurseries off Baja, California" was also a specialist subject. I also knew that you pronounced it BaHa as the Spanish used a J for an H, rather than like the striped woodland animal.

I knew the route of Offa's Dyke intimately, built by the erstwhile and eponymous King of Mercia. I knew where on the route one could catch, "glimpses of the silvern Wye as it meandered, gurgling restlessly past Tintern Abbey, much beloved of the romantic poets." As for the Romantic poets though, I could not name one.

I even checked in the dictionary to find out what eponymous meant and tried to work it into one conversation a week for the next month. Unfortunately, it seemed I was the only one who knew what eponymous meant and the second time I wove it casually into a sentence Ginger Rodney smacked me in the mouth for being a smartarse. Which I suppose was fair enough really.

I didn't like having Tuesday off as Tuesday was Andy Pandy day. I didn't like Andy Pandy because he dressed like a clown and I didn't like clowns. Clowns were either all forehead with red grimaces or patronising like adults, talking down to you in a high pitched voice. I particularly disliked the clown with the pointed hat, white face and saxophone. I didn't find him or his saxophone remotely funny.

Andy Pandy was also incredibly wet, mincing around like a puppet. I didn't like his equally wet and flat girlfriend Looby Lou either. They were made for each other. Ted was all right though, being a teddy bear and being called Ted, always looking for trouble – solid citizen.

I was fascinated by the garden scene at the beginning of Bill and Ben the Flowerpot men and found their inane banter very entertaining. Had I been the farmer, I'd have come out early from my dinner, sprayed Weed with insecticide and sold the Flowerpot Men to a travelling circus as a novelty act to replace the clowns. I realised it would be cruel to do that to Bill and Ben but it would mean a generation would not be subjected to clowns because, as I believe I mentioned, I do not like clowns.

Tales of the Riverbank was good. I liked the characters, rats, hamsters and guinea pigs. I simply thought it improbable that Roddy the water rat would have the finances, or the communication skills, to purchase a miniature speedboat for motoring up the river. Even if we could accept that he was an exceptionally gifted water rat who had come into an inheritance, a speedboat for an animal designed to move quickly through water seemed a bizarre purchase. It was like a Canada goose purchasing an aeroplane, or a trout buying a submarine. How would the other animals react to this vulgar display of wealth? If his river was anything like our estate, the local stoat would probably give him a smack for getting ideas above his station. Which I'd have to concede, would be fair enough really.

Friday was best as Friday meant the Woodentops. The Woodentop family were fine as far as wooden characters went but what really made the programme was Spot, "the biggest spotty dog in the whole world." I loved his little stiff-legged walk and his ability to cause mayhem.

Every week, the family would place the sausages on the table for dinner and every week Spot would snaffle the whole string of them when they weren't looking. The whole family would be befuddled on a weekly basis by the disappearance of the sausages and, in the end, they'd work out that Spot had probably eaten them. I got as far as getting out my fountain pen to write to the producers of the show...

Dear Woodentop Producers,

If they don't want Spot to eat the sausages tell the Woodentop family to stop putting them on the kitchen table and then leaving the room every week....

I thought better of it in the end. I did write to Blue Peter about my rabbit Snowy though and got a Blue Peter badge by return of post. Pleased as I was with the badge, I chose not to mention it on the Reso, as watching Blue Peter was not really something to be owned up to and writing letters was definitely one to keep hidden. I inadvertently wore it to school one day then had a terrible job convincing everyone that I had nicked it from one of the posh lads.

On one occasion my creative malingering did catch up with me though. That weekend I'd bought an Airfix aeroplane kit which was my usual investment whenever I had any pocket money, at the time. I'd shoot into town and fetch up at Poole's, an unusual shop which was part knitting wool emporium and part model shop. I'd be left to browse in the musty model shop while Mrs Poole attended to the needs of her discerning embroidery clients.

The shop had bags of the series one kits on a rotating stand and I would finger through them to find any new releases. On the shelving behind the counter were the series three and four kits, the Avro Lancasters, Flying Fortresses, Bismarcks and Ark Royals which were out of reach, literally and financially, on all but a birthday or Christmas.

I was content with the series one kits and two weeks worth of pocket money could be converted into one of these two shilling kits. I'd started by collecting aircraft and then diversified into military vehicles and I now had regiments of all the vehicles and at least one model of most of the aircraft. But there was always one more to collect and I'd chosen an obscure Italian fighter of the Second World War.

For some reason I was unable to complete the construction of the kit on the Saturday afternoon, which was my regular pattern, and building it was one of the features for my Friday off that week. It was easier to bunk Fridays as, once you had got through the initial hours between 7.30 and 9.00a.m., by which time I should have been at school, there was no need to lay the artifice on too heavily, as it was now practically the weekend anyway – three days in which to slowly recuperate.

With such thoughts in mind, and my mum resolved to conceding the day, by ten, I was up in my dressing gown and setting up my modelling place on the table, careful to cover the polished dark wood table with newspaper. It was dank and miserable outside, a bleak October day with rain and scudding clouds, and the fire was well stoked, making me feel warm and content. I thought of my friends pondering over some impenetrable mental maths problem related to two cars setting off at the same time at different speeds and the need to calculate the point at which they passed. I shuddered momentarily and burst open the plastic bag containing the Fiat fighter plane which would occupy me for the next hour.

Something strange always gripped me when I made an Airfix kit. It was an assembly line mentality, a need to get the model complete in the shortest time possible, the desire to see the finished article was so strong. I glanced quickly at the exploded construction diagram, noting only those points that were different from other similar kits I had made. My fingers worked feverishly, detaching the individual elements from the sprue. Wheels, propeller and wings yielded easily, but the scissors were needed for the smaller, more delicate articles.

I dry fitted the fuselage together, making sure the lugs engaged, and separated the two halves to apply glue. The tube of glue was always a potentially hazardous element in the procedure. It either ran too freely, scorching and melting the plastic, or not at all, at which point I'd have to apply pressure on it by rolling it like a toothpaste tube.

The glue ran a little too freely over the fuselage half and I cursed it as I lay it down to fit the halves together. They were setting nicely when I realised I had omitted the pilot seat and that, once the fuselage was assembled, it would be impossible to fit it. I quickly parted the fuselage halves and they yielded like sticky toffee. I reached again for the glue to dab a small blob on the lug to place the pilot seat. Done swiftly, I could have the seat in and the fuselage back together before the plastic deformed and was good for nothing. No glue came, so I ratcheted up the tube a turn to apply more pressure. Again no glue. I reached for the pin that I used to unclog the nozzle of the tube on such occasions and found it a minute later in the fold of the newspaper.

The model was beginning to warp and sag, within seconds it would resemble no more than the remains of a crashed plane, I was beside myself that my hard won pocket money could be wasted in such a way. I applied firm pressure to the tube, unaware that my probing with the pin had ruptured the side of the tube. As a volcano, finding, by a path of least resistance, a new vent so the glue erupted at ninety degrees to my purpose, arcing upwards in a jet that sprayed straight into my eyes.

It took a second for the accident to register but all at once my eyes were sealed by the thick glue and it began to burn into the inside of my eyelids and over my eyeballs.

At first all breath seemed to be extinguished from me, such was the pain and horror of the feeling. I remembered hyperventilating for a second, thinking that I could replay the unfurling events again, with greater care and less impatience, but it was not to be and with all dignity departing, I was screaming alternately for my mum and for God to help me. My vision in my left eye was now completely gone where my eyelids had sealed, my right eye had only the faintest blurry burning sensation. I noticed my voice had risen several octaves and I struggled with breathing and trying to describe succinctly to my mother what had happened as the adrenalin of fear coursed through me.

I'd never experienced pain like this. My previous worst had been the ear infection, and falling face forwards off a tricycle whilst taking a corner to fast.

This was of a different order altogether, in both those circumstances I could rationalise the pain. They had both hurt tremendously but the fear had been containable. Today, in the comfort of my own home, I believed I had blinded myself permanently.

The left eye was welded shut now, concentrating the glue on the inner surface of my eyelid and no amount of muscle movement on my part could dislodge it. The vision in my right eye was fading fast and I desperately tried to take in as much of my surroundings and my mum as I could before the darkness descended. My comfortable back room would afford me the last view I would have of the world.

Although she was there guiding me to the kitchen and bathing my eyes with milk and water, I still called for her and for God.

For five of the longest minutes of panic, the situation became graver and then the combination of my tears and the neutralising effect of the milk and water meant that my left eye reopened with a tearing that was like the thickest of sleep lodged in my eye, only infinitely worse.

Each eyelash needed to part from its neighbour and it took me at least a dozen attempts before I could manage to open my eye fully. Even then the vision in both eyes was grossly blurred and I consoled myself that I would navigate the world in shadow rather than total

darkness. This did not abate my tears, which was probably a good thing as they further diluted the glue and began to
lubricate my eye, which up to that point had been fitted with a cataract of congealing polystyrene cement.

At the best of times, I could not stand anything or anyone tampering with my eyes, and the next hour was an ordeal in which my eyes were drenched with warm olive oil, cold tea and milk in an effort to drain off the worst of the cement. When, after an hour, the pain had subsided to excruciating, I finally viewed myself in the kitchen mirror. My eyes were bloodshot and reddened, my eyelids swollen and stained with tea and olive oil but I could see, imperfectly.

My mum, having shared the panic, had now subsided into calm. She was smiling. She said, "It was interesting that you called for God as well as me." I remembered my direct prayer to the Almighty.

"Oh God, please don't let me go blind."

Which I had repeated several times and in my head my inner voice had added, "and I promise not to do anything bad ever again if you will just help me this once!" How many such direct and urgent calls must God receive each day, I now wondered. My mother was pleased that the crisis had brought with it such firm religious conviction on my part. I had to concede the point, God had seemed very real that day.

The trauma of that morning meant that I was now more than happy to assume the position of an invalid, which I had been so keen to avoid earlier in the day. I sat motionless looking out of the window at the bellicose day, sipping warm milky tea and savouring the sight of the wind blown leaves with inordinate satisfaction.

Just after midday my mother turned on the television to view the news. I was happy to view anything with my new lust for sight and was content to know that within the hour I'd be watching the Woodentops, God was back in his Heaven and, apart from the residual pain in my burning eyes, all was well with the world.

Within minutes the programme was interrupted by a stark screen bearing the words News Flash. I knew this was deeply ominous as the last time I had seen this sign was when Winston Churchill had died in 1965, and the time before that had been an evening's viewing of Bonanza interrupted by the events of November 1963. Nevertheless, I was almost excited at the potential of the forthcoming announcement – what could it be.

Seconds passed and the black and white screen flickered to a studio where a clearly shaken newscaster announced that in South Wales a terrific disaster had occurred when a coal tip, which was so characteristic of the area, and that of the adjoining valley where my mum's family lived, had, during heavy rains, slipped and engulfed the village of Aberfan.

I read this to mean that the village had mud and coal dust in the streets, but when they cut from the studio to the outside broadcast unit, the full horror of the situation hit. This had not been a stream of mud but an avalanche of enormous proportions, a tsunami of glutinous black mud whose first victim had been the local primary school.

It was now just after midday and despite the frantic efforts of local rescuers, no people had been rescued alive for an hour. It was known that there were almost one hundred and fifty children and teachers entombed in the school. Entombed was unfortunately not hyperbole, as the level of the mud on the walls of the school and the feverish activity of the would-be rescuers testified.

A wave of guilt struck me at this point. Having skived the day off school and self -inflicted a temporary blindness on myself, had I, in my panic, distracted God at a time when there were more worthy calls on His time in South Wales? It was years later, when I learned that God was meant to be omnipotent, all seeing and all knowing, that I was able to lay down some of the guilt of that day. For at the time that I was screaming for my sight, which was hastily restored, twelve score young souls were battling in vain for their lives.

I resolved never to take time off school in this manner again, and never to distract God when he clearly had more important business to attend to. The following February, on the second day of the snow and despite my best intentions, I woke up feeling weak and feeble and convinced my mum it was the onset of flu.

Chapter Eighteen
SHAME

On the long summer nights the clinic field was the place to gather. Several acres of playing field punctuated only by two sets of hockey posts and a further two sets of football posts. We could let off steam here and not get in anyone's way.

Technically, the clinic field was closed, surrounded by a seven foot high metal railing fence. The only official entrances were where the teams moved through a gate with a barbed wire top near to the changing rooms and the gates where the tractor, with its trailing mowing blades, entered once a fortnight to keep the grass in tip- top condition.

This being the Reso, within a couple of days of the fencing being erected, the local residents had tired of making the trek to one corner of the field, climbing up on the wall of the clinic and jumping eight feet down into the playing area. Someone, nobody knew who, applied sufficient pressure on the metal railings to bend them and allow an awkward access into the field. A second feat of strength at the opposite diagonal, meant that a permanent pathway was created off the estate and leading, by the shortest route, into the town for the use of children and parents alike.

Some said that Woody had bent the bars with his bare hands. It certainly would not have been beyond Woody who, at the age of twelve, already had hairy arms and rippling muscles bursting out of over-developed biceps. Woody was a useful ally to have and I did my best to keep in with him. When asked about it he smiled and said nothing, which was very cool of him. Whether I'd done it or not, if asked, I'd have claimed it as my handiwork. Which, I suppose, was why I was not as cool as Woody. Everyone would know that I had not done it because I was too keen to claim the kudos. Woody with his biceps and his silence left an element of doubt.

Others claimed that a parent had done it. This was a possibility but it would have been strange for a parent to have done something so positively useful for all the children of the estate. Perhaps it was someone too lazy to walk round or someone desperate to shorten the journey to the nearest pub. On one or other of these two counts many dads qualified. It might have been a dad sick of us playing in the street and disrupting sleep after a long night shift. That sounded reasonable, and again many dads would fit the bill on this count.

It could not have been someone too fat as, even for me, the squeeze through was quite tight and for anyone larger it would have been a wasted effort.

When I pondered the thought in bed, on the eve of sleep, I imagined a circus strongman, dressed like Fred Flintstone in an animal skin leotard striding purposefully to the fence accompanied by clowns playing circus music. The strongman, with a black handlebar moustache and greased back hair would turn to the assembled crowd, flex his biceps, Popeye style, and yank the bars apart in a single strain and would take the adulation of the crowd to a musical Taaa – Raaa!

Whatever the cause, we had now established the new traditional route into town, and in all the time I lived on the Reso I don't remember a single occasion when a visit to town did not mean sidling through the bars of the clinic field.

On this particular summer's night, we had played our fifty a side football match with all the usual crew. Some of the older lads had attended this early evening session before preparing themselves for a Saturday night's prowling the promenade and the fair for this week's crop of girls. Even pigeon-toed Tommy Aspinall had joined us for the game in the improbable kit of winkle pickers and drain pipe jeans. In between attending to his Brylcreemed quiff he'd make a cursory charge for the ball if it came within ten yards of him.

Unfortunately, his footwear ensured that in the unlikely event of his making contact with the ball it would slice off in any unpredictable direction but never straight and never to a member of his team. Brazil it wasn't. Tommy would immediately stop, unperturbed, and resume his grooming with his metal comb, which he had honed to a shark's tooth edge, "just in case."

Tommy's plan, should he be caught out on the mean and gaudily illuminated streets leading up to the promenade, was to whip out his razor-edged comb and see off all-comers. At this moment of intense grooming, though, he managed to take the yellow head off a particularly ripe boil on his temple. It was probably the only blood letting action the comb would ever see. As the blood trickled down his face and splattered onto his floral print shirt, Tommy was off in a pigeon-toed flurry cursing and calling.

The secret in these games was to get rid of the ball as quickly as possible before the hordes descended on you. With an acre to play in, all but the two goalkeepers, one of whom was 'Rush' and a couple of the dodgy lads who merely lolloped near the opponents' goal and talked, everyone was in a wildebeest frenzy of kick and rush no more than an arm's distance from four opponents. There were times when we lost sight of the ball and merely piled into a heap until the ball, with a life of its own, squirmed out from the melee and set us all off again pell-mell in random directions.

Larry, as only Larry could, made the mistake of positioning himself out on what approximated the wing, next to the railing fence. The other wing extended almost four hundred yards across the pitch. With no referee or linesman to adjudicate when the ball was out of play, we merely kept legging it further and further from the goals. Only the Campini brothers could decide when the line had been crossed, and if they shouted "out" you merely picked up the ball and gave it to them whether it was their throw or not, or risked the consequences.

Larry waited patiently for the scrums to develop and the ball to cannonade out to him. He waited in vain for the best part of an hour until the ball finally fell at his feet. He built up some momentum and when confronted by Ginger Rodney, played a deft one-two off the railings, leaving a disgruntled mop of ginger hair in his wake. In his stride now, the ball caressed at his feet, he looked up and measured an inch perfect cross into the path of four would be centre forwards. He slowed to a stop and admired the curved flight of the leather ball streaming part of its lace against a clear blue sky. He did not witness the outcome of his cross as instantaneously three of his opponents careered him into the railings, winding him and leaving him with nasty railing size welts across his back. Over the coming days, as the bruises developed and subsided he looked as if he was standing behind a vertical Venetian blind.

Larry, Larry, Larry, when would he ever learn – the same thing had happened to him the week before and no doubt would re-occur over the span of that balmy summer. His big mistake was in believing he was playing football according to the rules of the Football Association, to the standards demanded by FIFA. He was playing Reso football, which was a fish from a completely different kettle. Reso football was vengeance with an incidental ball, a time to settle scores and to bond.

When we had finished laughing at limping, sobbing Larry, dragging his sorry carcass off home, a lull settled on the game and the older lads sidled off to prepare for their night on the promenade, strutting and preening, and intimidating the visitors.

In one of the goals, a proper game of heads and volleys developed with five and "in". The only problem was that nobody wanted to be goalie when the misplaced headers and volleys inevitably meant more time than not was spent retrieving the ball from the road and passing an inordinate number of times through the gap in the bars to get it.

We spent the next half hour thinking up and rejecting things to do to amuse ourselves. There was little consensus. Martin wanted to play Marathon, an unimaginative game where we ran around the perimeter of the field until we dropped out through exhaustion, one by one. The last one standing was acclaimed as Champion. There was not much enthusiasm for this suggestion as on the three previous times we had been coaxed into this game, iron-lunged Martin was still lapping the field when all the rest of us had gone home to bed exhausted and sweat drenched.

I don't know how he managed it but he did have a beautifully economical running style and a metronomic pace which he was able to maintain indefinitely, it seemed.

I could not resist setting off at a sprint, overtaking lads who were older and stronger than me, basking in early and short lived glory, only to be reeled in after a lap and a half as my energy sapped away and my mental spirit collapsed like a sandcastle in the tide.

A suggestion of Grand National gained few takers given the events of earlier in the summer. Even the truncated version, where we set up a number of steeplechase hurdles in the field from the mown grass and created a treacherous water jump by peeing in the six foot span beyond the grass clipping hedge, hoping that someone, other than me, would land short and slip on the dewy urine splattered grass, found few takers. It would take too long to gather the grass and we were all too dehydrated from the football to do justice to the creation of the water jump.

A few more of our group drifted off to see the latest edition of Batman on the tele. I was left with Ronnie and the old fall back of

True, Dare, Kiss, Command, Promise. He had given me a bit of a verbal going over recently, so I studiously avoided True, Kiss and Promise. We tossed for start and he, with his magic coin, or knowing that I would be too afraid to contradict him, won.

I thought I was relatively safe with Command. Command usually meant doing something and, although Ronnie would look carefully for something which would put me in physical danger or would cause embarrassment to my parents, at least it would not involve another verbal humiliation in front of my friends. Ronnie was very good at that – too good.

He seemed to read the things about which I was most sensitive. I knew he sometimes engaged me in seemingly aimless conversations just to probe my weaknesses. Would I prefer someone to wee on my trousers or spit on my back? Would I prefer to be called Lanky or Spasmo? I tried to answer neither but he'd press me with, "Yeah, but if your life depended on it which would you prefer?"

I noticed he looked too carefully at me as I answered. He was looking for a twitch or my face flushing. This was not idle curiosity, it was a full-scale interrogation. Sure enough, the things that I had shown the greatest aversion to would be visited on me in the coming weeks or months, sometimes a year later when I'd forgotten what I had let slip. He'd take particular glee in sharing my fears with others in the group and, like sharks smelling blood, I'd quickly be surrounded and humiliated by the frenzy.

I'd tried to put him off the scent by answering the opposite to what I really thought. Sensing my deception, he had quickly moved on to a game of, "Yes means No and No means Yes."

"Do you want a Chinese burn – five seconds to answer?"

He'd count down in a measured way.

Whatever the answer, I knew a Chinese burn was inevitable. If I answered yes I'd get a Chinese burn and he would state that he was genuinely alarmed that I'd volunteer for such a painful experience when all I had to do was say no.

If I answered, "No," he'd patiently reiterate the rules of the game and express surprise that I found it so hard to grasp then grab my arm in a vicelike grip and twist for all he was worth. I didn't cry though, not then or ever, and that was my one consolation. He'd never make me cry. I might be trembling with panic inside but I always managed to remain stony-faced.

However, Ronnie did have the satisfaction of knowing that he could visit any manner of torture or indignity on me and that I'd never grass him up. I could never take that road. So any number of passing Tanzanians, Russians or Bulgarians took the blame for the succession of welts, bruises, cuts and bloody noses with which I often made my way home.

Ronnie looked around idly seeking a sufficient indignity for me. I winced in anticipation. To my surprise his gaze moved to the far side of the field where Paul was sitting quietly with some of his mates.

Paul lived in the railway terrace, not the estate proper. He was a talented musician whose family had a piano and an accordion in the house, and Paul was learning, quite successfully, to play the latter. He was a frenzy of bellows and octopus fingers coaxing the semblance of a tune out of the squeeze box. He once let me have a try without my asking, trusting me with this precious family artefact. All I could summon from the box of delights was a whine that sounded like an approximation of a semi-melodic fart. This would have played particularly well on the Reso, but I felt disappointed and crest-fallen by my paltry effort at creating music in Paul's house.

We often sat together in school because he was a good artist and could show me how to draw and paint beyond my stick people and daubing style. He seemed to have endless patience to go with his good humour.

I'd once, at the start of a discussion about an essay on My Family, volunteered the phrase "consists of" to Mr Jones the Adjective. Mr Jones, in true Celtic style, went into raptures about this reaching for the 'mot juste' as he called it – the avoidance of the lazy and the obvious. Paul had then trumped me with the single word 'comprises' and Jones the Adjective found a new level of ecstasy and immediately awarded him a housemark, striking it down on his desk in an overly theatrical gesture.

I really admired Paul in that moment for conjuring up such a word. He did it again the following week when he volunteered 'donned' for the action of putting on a coat. I'd never heard of it but Jones the Adjective was once again on cloud nine. I thought he was going to adopt Paul, such was his enthusiasm for his angelic vocabulary in that second. Such things counted for a lot in Wales. I found out just how much it meant to Jones the Adjective when we attended the local Eisteddfod the following year and there was Jones, looking like some Druidic Arab Sheik, as pleased, if not as good-looking, as Punch, receiving a Bardic Chair for some poetry he had written.

I'd spent many a happy hour in the railway allotments behind Paul's house sampling the peas in their pods and hunting grasshoppers and ant nests on the one, long-abandoned allotment. All this furious activity took place, to the backdrop of 41220, my favourite shunting engine, idly shuffling coal wagons and vans around the fan of sidings whilst the expresses galloped through the main station.

"You see that Paul over there?" said Ronnie disdainfully, "You've got to kidnap him and hold him prisoner for me."

Initially I was relieved. It was a do-able command and if I let Paul in on it, it would be easily achievable. But I quickly realised that I could not let Paul in on it. He was of a nervous disposition at the best of times and, out of fear, he never entered the Reso proper unless coming directly to my house with his mum standing on the polished, red tiles of her terrace doorstep watching him every step of the way across the clinic field.

I toyed with alternatives for a second: appease Ronnie and betray Paul, or stand up to Ronnie. There was no contest. To my shame, fear made me choose the first, and wrong, alternative. I snaked my way over the field to Paul, careful to disguise my point of origin with Ronnie. I engaged him in conversation and mentioned an Airfix kit, another passion we had in common, that I was having trouble with and asked him if he would quickly check it out for me. He was as reluctant as I was insistent but he made his way over to my house imploring that it should take no more than five minutes, and glancing nervously back to his empty doorstep.

Once he had squeezed through the railings he had no quick way back home. I could outrun him and overpower him. I continued my deception but I sensed his unease. In a single movement I bundled him over the crenulated brickwork of Ronnie's garden wall and onto his lawn where, with me sitting astride him, he was completely invisible to any concerned mothers scouring the horizon from a quarter of a mile away. I thought Paul, and Jones the Adjective, would have appreciated crenulated or castellated, but in faith, Paul was beyond appreciating anything, his face was an asthmatic red and he was beginning to cry panic-stricken tears.

"Good work," said Ronnie, "keep him there until I come back."

Ronnie entered his house through the side gate and I immediately tried to reassure Paul that no harm would come to him. We both knew it was a hollow promise as I'd been scared enough to kidnap him on the word of Ronnie and even with Ronnie gone indoors, I still found I had not relaxed my constrictor grip on Paul's chest.

He started to beg me to release him through his tears. I tried to calm him but at no point did I release my grip, such was my fear of Ronnie's retribution.

After ten minutes Paul was hyperventilating, his face a red, blubbering, and swollen mess. I thought that he would settle down after a few minutes but he simply panicked further. I suddenly came to my senses and released him. He was exhausted by the struggle and unable even to get up at first. I was now keen to get him away from Ronnie's and back home as quickly as possible. I knew the torture would be redoubled on both of us if Ronnie came out of his house at this moment.

I got Paul out of the garden, across the road and through the railings. I thought he would cheer up and compose himself now, as he was in sight of home, but he had been so disturbed by the experience that he still needed my support to make his way home. On that balmy summer's evening, anyone who had seen us might have come to the quite false conclusion that I was a Good Samaritan who was shepherding a good friend home. In my fear of the wrath of Ronnie, I had visited on Paul exactly the retribution that Ronnie regularly visited on me. It mattered not one iota to Paul what my motivation had been, the experience had been a wretched one for him and one, if his continued blubbering was to be believed, that would leave a lasting and damaging impression on him.

I thought of all the good times we had shared together and the times he had helped me in school and I felt deeply ashamed of my cowardly actions. I said sorry repeatedly, but I doubt Paul heard me. He was confined in a mask of snot and tears. I felt the reproachful look of my mum boring into the back of my head and the scratching in red in the debit column of the Big Book for my shameful part in this night's events.

I ushered him through the second set of railings and across the road to his terrace of houses. I left him there to make his own way the last twenty five yards to his front door.

I was too scared to have to explain to his mother what had happened to him and my part in it. I hid round the side alleyway and watched as his mother bundled him in and then ran back across the clinic field before she could arrange a posse to lynch me. I wondered if Paul might say nothing directly about my involvement: the code of the Reso.

I realised I didn't deserve his protection after the way I had betrayed his trust. Whatever his mum might or might not do to me was as nothing compared to the damage I had done to my so-called friend. I realised that the good times we had shared were at an end. I could not expect Paul to trust me again after this.

Although I was not crying, inside I was in turmoil. Despite this and compounding my shame, I returned to Ronnie's garden and, when he emerged half an hour later, having casually forgotten we were there, I feigned that Paul had hit me when I had not expected it and escaped, so as to cover my miserable yellow back from Ronnie's retribution.

Paul was able to exact a terrible retribution on me over the coming months. He simply did not speak to me. He moved out of any group, room, table or dinner queue that I entered. I tried, on numerous occasions, to apologise, hoping that when the heat went out of the memory, things could return to normal, but they never did and when we did eventually speak there was always a distance between us. I never again enjoyed making his concertina fart, or chasing grasshoppers round the allotment with trains thundering by.

As for Ronnie, my resentment against him festered. Several months later, having played the Yes means No game once too often, he got me in a leg lock around my chest and applied the usual steady pressure so that he could hear me say, "Submit."

I'd never taken any opportunity to retaliate, fearing further retribution, but this night I managed to roll onto my right side and leave my left hand free. For once I did not hold back and levered myself so that my arm described a wide purposeful arc with my fist landing with considerable force on the bridge of Ronnie's nose. He screamed, as much in surprise as pain, as a rosette of scarlet burst from his nose. He rolled over to cover his nose and the tears came freely.

His mother, alerted by his repeated screams, emerged from the kitchen door to find Ronnie pole-axed on the ground and me looking steadfast and triumphant over him.

"Whatever has happened?" she exclaimed.

I did not move, speak or attempt to explain and it was left to Ronnie to cry, "He hit me!"

Still I did not move, despite Ronnie's mum's remonstrations. I stood still as she helped him up and I made sure he had ample opportunity to see my face, not twitching and cowed but still and determined, as he limped past me.

After that, things were never the same between Ronnie and me, thankfully. In that action I had broken the spell of intimidation that he had held over me for so many years. But I could take little satisfaction in that because it had cost me Paul's friendship to summon up the courage to challenge him.

I could not even seek solace in the idea that I had broken the will of a bully and rendered a public service. For a bully was probably exactly how Paul now viewed me.

Chapter Nineteen
PLUMMET

It was about this time that I suddenly got interested in girls. Up until now I had had very little to do with girls. They were either cousins, or got in the way when you were playing football in the playground. Other than that, I had been left largely indifferent to them except for Tilly and Marilyn, who were particularly well developed physically and who were vaguely threatening on account of the fact that they could run almost as fast as me.

I liked the potential of replying to the question, "Have you got a girlfriend?" with a nonchalant, "Yes, I've got a girlfriend – hasn't everybody?"

What use I might have for a girlfriend was less clear. She could watch me play football or skim stones, she may even like to join me for train spotting perhaps, or maybe not.

So when I was busy doing other things, I suddenly developed the need to acquire a girlfriend. How to do this was the next question. Could you just shuffle up to one of the nicer girls in school and by being seen around with her enough become the boyfriend. God forbid that you actually had to go up to her and ask her to become your girlfriend – far too risky.

"Excuse me Debbie, I can see you are busy with your friends at the moment but I was wondering, hoping might be a better word, that you might like to, to… what I'm trying to say is do you want to be my girlfriend?"

Debbie would look at me, astonished at my effrontery, and having taken a millisecond to weigh up the proposal would simply answer, "No."

I would walk away humiliated in front of all the girls and would later claim that it was some other lad, who had been going round impersonating me but whom I could not identify.

Perhaps you could arrange it by correspondence:

Dear Susan,

I've admired you from afar for some time now and was wondering if you would like to become my girlfriend. The post will not take up too much of your time and would involve you sharing some of my hobbies and sometimes walks. You must also be prepared to say that I am your boyfriend if anyone asks.
Yours sincerely,
David
RSVP
PS No kissing or sloppy stuff involved.

A touch formal perhaps, but I thought it right to set out what was involved. This would be a big step up from the usual, "Sharon fancies you! She doesn't know I sent this note," notes that would circulate around class. You'd look up to see Sharon all limp hair, spots and thick glasses staring at you like a desperate rabbit with myxomatosis. You knew she had sent the note as a line of faces was staring at you showing the people who had passed the note on, reading it quickly and giggling before doing so.

My distinctive writing meant that this approach too had problems as it would be difficult to deny having written the letter, and it constituted evidence with which to torture me in future. I saw myself in a circle of tormenting girls throwing my letter in the form of a paper dart between them, always just out of my reach.

An approach which I had seen work had been to get a trusted mate to propose for you whilst you desperately appeared to look rugged and athletic, playing sport and being preoccupied. That way you could always deny all knowledge of the proposal. This might have worked, although I did not have any trusted friends. I knew, had I been put in the position of trusted friend, I could not stop myself from wringing the maximum embarrassment factor out of this one.

I could imagine myself yelling from one end of the playground to the other, "Andy, mate, I've asked her to go out with you and she said never in a million years," and, as an afterthought, I'd add, "Sorry mate!"

Clearly, I would have to get a girlfriend by stealth. A casual conversation, "You going to the swimming baths this weekend?" If the answer was yes spend the whole weekend at the baths looking to engineer a chance encounter. Arrive back at school on Monday decidedly cleaner and with fingers still shrivelled from spending too much time in chlorine filled pool.

"Didn't see you at the baths this weekend," I'd venture, excessively casually.

"No I went out with my boyfriend instead."

Thwarted!

So the chance of a double date with Ted and a girl he fancied, Julie, seemed an ideal compromise. On the downside, I did not know who I would end up with. On a more positive note, I could walk away with dignity intact, no notes, no commitments.

It turned out to be Janet, which really was a mixed blessing. On the one hand a number of the lads fancied her, on the downside she was generally dismissive of boys – being able to arm wrestle at least two thirds of the boys in the class. I was more than a little scared of her.

I was reasonably relieved that Julie and Janet had such low expectations of us as 'boyfriends' as we set off for our walk down the promenade that Saturday.

They suggested we buy them candy floss and a drink of Tizer, which we did. They also made it clear that they did not consider this as a full date, which suited me, with my mixed feelings about Janet. They then proceeded to walk three paces behind us for most of the length of the promenade. I was happy enough but I could see that Ted was rattled as he was particularly keen on Julie and was looking to spend at least a few brief minutes with her alone.

I had tried to engage the girls in conversation on a host of very interesting topics, only for them to swat my efforts like a troublesome fly and return to their engrossing conversation. I had run on to the beach and demonstrated my prowess at skimming stones, managing a niner on my second attempt only to turn in triumph to find them fifty yards down the promenade still talking incessantly and oblivious to my achievement. I raced back to join them to find a glum Ted, and the girls both talking and listening at the same time in the way that only girls do.

It seemed I would have to do something quite spectacular to break the girls' conversation and give Ted his in with Julie. By now I was getting a little miffed at their clear lack of interest in our presence. It struck at the heart of our credibility as lads.

Dogged by the irrepressible urge to appear interesting, brave and whimsical all at the same time, and lacking any words to express these qualities, I fell upon a physical demonstration of my character. I'd casually jump off the twenty-five foot sea wall onto the sand below. The girls would be so impressed and Ted, lacking the courage to follow suit, would make my achievement all the more impressive.

On reflection, I should have tried one of these qualities at a time and chosen something less ambitious, or perhaps added stupidity to the list. In my favour, I knew the sea wall well and the quality of the sand at each point. However, I had never jumped from this point before, as I had always considered it too high and dangerous. The secret this time was not to dwell too much on the task in hand. Nothing could be worse than to climb over the guardrail and stand there rocking back and forth as if winding up the clockwork mechanism that was courage, to the point that you could jump, only to think better of it and scurry back over the rail, crestfallen.

Far better to run at the guardrail, leap over it and nonchalantly disappear from view.

"Do it, do it now," whispered the insistent voice in my head which was not my mum's.

I turned to the girls, walking arm in arm and intent on some conversation about who had said what to whom and when and shouted, "Catch you later ladies!" and set off on my run. The girls glanced momentarily across in my direction then resumed their conversation, their backs towards my extraordinary feat. I accelerated over the guardrail and began my downward arc.

I used the brief time spent plummeting off a twenty-five foot sea wall to impress a potential girlfriend to realise it was probably a hideous mistake. I listened attentively for the shattering of bone which would mark the end of my descent. I realised the high tide, that has just receded, had flattened and compacted the normally golden sand at this point to the consistency of concrete. To compound the misery, and possibly my injuries, the tide had scoured the sand to a mere couple of inches, revealing real and unforgiving concrete underneath.

I landed with a dull crump that winded me. The inability to breathe did at least stem the pain from every joint in my body. The pain was so intense from so many places at once that I decided just to lie still whilst my brain shuffled the broken bones into an order of seriousness.

I'd been there for about twenty seconds when Ted appeared over the rail and asked, as if he expected a coherent answer, "What did you do that for?" I toyed with the truth, to impress a girl; a whimsical answer, to see if I could fly; a brave one, to laugh in the face of death. The voice in my head, which was not my mum's, and which had been so enthusiastic seconds before, cut in with the correct answer,

"Because you are a prat."

I made a mental note not to listen to that voice again. Unfortunately, when it arrived at the voice's address, he immediately tore it up.

Chapter Twenty
DECADE

Although I started the decade believing that the most exciting night of the year was Christmas Eve, I ended it in December 1969, knowing it to be New Year's Eve. It was all part of growing up really, giving up the childlike pleasures for a glimpse of the possibilities of adulthood.

For some reason which I could not fathom, my parents, who were not known to be particularly gregarious adults during the rest of the year, always hosted a New Year's Eve party. This had become a tradition and a variety of real and pretend aunties and uncles and family friends would wend their unsteady way to our front door as the midnight hour approached in each year of the 1960s.

The first to arrive were always Aunties Mary and Glad. Firm friends of my mum's since school days, they came round every Tuesday evening and sat chatting and drinking tea whilst my dad attempted to watch the television with the sound down. The Tuesday get-togethers had gone on since before my birth and the aunties always arrived on the dot of eight o'clock. Auntie Mary always brought a tube of Smarties for me and I'd accept them graciously and then proceed to eat them quickly before using the tube to launch the plastic end cap. I had complete alphabets of the Smartie tube tops in different colours hidden away in the back of the second drawer in my bedroom.

The only problem with the aunties was that they smoked copiously – Players – like my dad, and when they all got going there was a furious fug in the room, which, combined with the draw of the coal fire, had you losing consciousness in minutes.

On New Year's Eve the aunties would be there by six and would set themselves with a port and lemon in the kitchen, deftly slicing finger rolls and making up egg mayonnaise and John West pink salmon and vinegar sandwiches. I'd be entranced and disgusted as Auntie Glad would smoke over the sandwiches and allow her ash to reach precarious proportions as she talked and coughed. Much as I was disgusted by smoking, I was determined to ensure that the sandwiches remained uncontaminated, as there was only Easter and Christmas when such fare could be sampled.

My dad would be busy opening the Watneys Red Barrel Party Bumpers – seven pints in a single tin which could go off like a mortar if not allowed to settle before opening. There were three red and three blue bumpers – mild and bitter both tasted diabolical to me and I could not really understand what all the fuss was about drinking beer.

In the cold of the pantry were the more exotic drinks, Harvey's Bristol Cream sherry, a ruby port, an ancient bottle of Navy Rum, a Teacher's whisky and the 'girly corner' drinks.

The latter consisted of a dozen Cherry B drinks, a dozen bottles of Babycham, a bottle of Vodka which went unopened from one year to the next and a large custard yellow bottle of Warninks Advocaat. For some reason I misread the bottle and thought it read Waltons and believed that, like our neighbours, Advocaat was a product of the Black Country. On the floor were half a dozen bottles of Mackeson's sweet stout for the ladies, like my nain, who liked to think of their drinking as medicinal.

Below the alcohol were Corona soft drinks of every hue, rich in artificial additives and cyclamates, a violent green lime, an overenthusiastic tango and an understated cream soda that always made my mouth foam in a way that only sherbet could replicate. These had been delivered by the bright yellow, purpose built, Commer lorry the day before. Why a lorry should be named after a punctuation mark was beyond me, but then again, why were all our local fire engines and dust carts called Dennis? I was very proud that, just once a year, the Corona van stopped at our gate, and disappointed to find that no one in the street witnessed it.

On New Year's Eve I often drank dandelion and burdock as it looked like beer, but it made me terribly windy and unable to speak coherently which, I was to learn later, was the effect I should have been aiming for.

From six to nine the aunties and my mum ploughed on with rolls and sandwiches. Certainly, more people were catered for than on the Sermon on the Mount. Anything not consumed would end up in my dad's snap tin over the coming days so nothing would be wasted.

My mum also busied herself with the angel cakes and her signature mandarin gateau and sherry trifle. She decorated the latter with hundreds and thousands and liberally completed the effect with little spheres which had the look and structural integrity of ball bearings. Anyone chomping down on them would be sure to dislodge a filling. It seemed such a bizarre additional ingredient to put into such a smooth and silky trifle and it was sure to catch some unwary eaters out. I made a mental note to keep a watch out for the first person to lose their fillings.

The girls would prattle on, deaf auntie Mary enunciating every syllable of what she said and Auntie Glad with the infuriating habit of trying to guess the last word of your sentence as you said it and then adding, "Yeeees" to the end of it. Invariably she would be wrong, but, undeterred, she'd blunder on to the end of your next sentence. She'd reduced listening to a kind of Bingo in which she never got remotely near an individual number right. In the end I'd give up and leave the room.

As the clock ticked beyond nine o'clock I'd try to distract myself so that I could keep myself awake until the party really kicked off. One year, I catnapped and woke at six o'clock the next morning to find the detritus of the party strewn over the house and my Uncle Freddie finishing off one of the party bumpers whilst my Auntie Sarah tried to convince him that they should head for home rather than outstay their welcome.

My mum would take advantage of my absence from the kitchen to arrange the nibbles in the peach coloured plastic sundae bowls. There were little cheese footballs and savoury biscuits in the form of letters from Marks and Sparks together with potato sticks with a vicious salt and vinegar flavour. TUC biscuits were liberally spread with cream cheese and grapefruits were wrapped in bacofoil and speared with sticks of cheese and cocktail sausages. I'd helped with this stage of the preparation one year but had been shooed out of the kitchen when it was realised I could consume said produce faster than the three of them could manufacture it.

Auntie Dorothy would be supplying copious amounts of sausage rolls and mince pies with short crust pastry, whilst Nain would bring a *Bara Brith*, a rich, malty fruit cake, traditional in Wales for high days, holidays and funerals.

My mum would have prepared enormous amounts of Welsh cakes earlier and packed them in the plastic containers from long digested ice cream. These Welsh cakes would be specially prepared on a griddle; fruity and sweet, I could consume them in biblical quantities when the mood took me, and it took me on a regular basis.

With me out of nose shot, the last dishes would be assembled. These would include Cadbury's chocolate finger biscuits and the frosted biscuits with hard orange and pink icing that I always associated with other people's birthday parties. These were kept out of my reach for now, but with the guests milling later I'd be able to fill a party plate and retreat under the front room table, safely hidden by a heavy linen table cloth that my mother had bleached to radiance.

Nine fifteen and still no guests had arrived. Uncle Jim had passed through in his bus driver jacket and cap looking like something between a middle European policeman and a seaside ice cream seller. His special official bus driver badge always appealed to me, as did the white fluorescent bands on the bottom of his sleeves. He had come, as he always did, to bring some records for later in the evening. He loved the rich tone of the mahogany radio gramophone that sat in the window alcove of our front room and would find any excuse to play his records on it.

He had rifled, as he always did, through our record collection with some disdain. First for rebuke was a traditional Christmas selection LP with a cover which looked as though a primary school had put it together from as many images of Christmas as could be mustered. Rudolph, holly, Christmas trees, presents, mince pies and a hearty Father Christmas were all there together with some less than seasonal girls dressed in exceptionally short red skirts and black high-heeled boots. Santa seemed to be eyeing them with more than usual interest. Little Drummer Boy, White Christmas, Nat King Cole with Mary's Boy Child and Rudolph the Red Nosed Reindeer all featured, as did some more religious music. Jim had cast it to the ground declaring it to be rubbish of the first order.

Next up were a selection of singles in flimsy paper covers bearing the labels of Parlophone, Decca and EMI. Glad All Over by the Dave Clark Five, which I'd battered the saucepans to for a number of years, was sniffed at and tossed aside, as was Diana Ross's invitation to sample some Baby Love with her Supremes. At least The Beatles' Love Me Do would strike a chord with Jim, I thought. I'd always associated it with the first time I'd seen The Beatles on television, in 1962, with John Lennon playing a fat acoustic guitar in his sharp suit, Paul and George standing to his right and only Paul's left handedness balancing up the shape of their guitars. "Love Me Do indeed," was Jim's only response.

The only thing that brought a smile to his eye was to delve among the 78 rpm records which had worked their way to the back of the gramophone storage area. From here he produced two favourites. First came the immortal song I've Got a Lovely Bunch of Coconuts!, which I always thought must have a deeper and dirtier meaning than the obvious one, as the adults always passed knowing glances and laughed whenever it was played. I hoped, in the fullness of time, to have a lovely bunch of coconuts myself, despite the fact that the only time I had ever handled and opened one it had felt like an old man's skull, and the liquid inside was foul. The flesh tasted of Bounty Bar and I despised Bounty Bars. It was only later that I found out they were actually made of coconut, which would probably explain a lot.

I added coconut to my list of food hates, finding little to differentiate it from all the other nuts on my list, the fish and the foreign food, and the Sunday dinners not cooked by my mum or my Nain.

The second record Jim approved of and played was Ronny Ronalde's In a Monastery Garden. This consisted of violins and what sounded like the flexed saw and bow I'd once seen Laurel and Hardy play, and some stupid discordant fool whistling over the top. The music always reminded me of cemeteries for some odd reason, and it clearly moved Jim deeply because tears streamed down his cheeks. His reddened face was so contorted I could not be sure whether he was laughing or crying. This alarmed me because the sight of men crying had, on the rare occasions I had witnessed it first hand, always portended no good – an illness or a death in the family.

To my relief, he eventually attempted to wipe his eyes and compose himself, and, although he spoke in the high pitched whine of the distressed, I could see his stomach rising and falling as he tried to control his laughter. He tried again to whistle in tune with Ronny and burst out laughing, this time setting off my mum who had entered the room, as perturbed as I had been at the kerfuffle.

She called on Aunty Bet to attend. She too burst into tears of laughter. Aunty Glad arrived some moments later as the laughter subsided and proceeded to whistle the tune – but always three notes behind the pace, which set us off again.

We stood there for no less than five minutes all laughing, unable to draw breath to speak, to the point that we could not remember what had set us off. I wanted this to go on for ever, but eventually, as always happened whenever I laughed myself senseless, I suddenly felt as empty and desolate as when I had watched the pathetic part of Norman Wisdom films, or saw the sadness in Stan Laurel's face, and I ended up crying sad tears.

For all his brashness, Uncle Jim was a man of hidden depths and culture. His record collection comprised exclusively classical music and he never missed either the Christmas concert of Lessons and Carols from King's College Cambridge or the Vienna Boy's Choir Concert broadcast over the BBC World Service at New Year. At great cost, he'd bought himself an early tape recorder to capture such concerts and it was this quality of sound that always drew him to our radiogram.

It was an ugly piece of mahogany furniture with an Art Deco cloth front and light wood overlaying it. The only other place I'd seen something similar to it in style was at the local Odeon where the plaster flanking the silver screen was done up in a similar design. It took three people to move the radiogram whenever we decorated, and this weight gave it a deep, mellow bass tone.

His eyes now dry, Uncle Jim carefully reached into the small case containing some pearls from his own collection. There was no surprise that the first record he produced was Five Thousand Welsh Voices Sing from the Royal Albert Hall.

This was a choral triumph with all the Welsh standard hymns and arias included.

My only question was why five thousand Welsh people had felt the need to travel to London to sing in their native language to a small audience (once they'd got the choirs in) of English speakers. It seemed unusually perverse to me. Ten Thousand Welsh Voices singing from Aberwystwyth seemed more sensible.

An hour of the walls resonating to *Sanctiadd* and *Calon Lan*, and Jim was sated and the rest of us aurally exhausted. He removed the record carefully and dabbed and polished it with an anti-static cleaning cloth he had bought from Greave's, the specialist record shop in the town.

"Right," he declared, "I'm off. See you later."

He muttered something in Auntie Glad's ear which made her scream and shudder with laughter and was off into the dark, dank night.

The girls, job done, retired to the living room and, despite the array of exotic drinks on show, opted for a nice cup of tea. I moved uneasily from the front door to the front window and back to the kitchen to see if I could snaffle some edibles, but was too excited to settle to anything. If I sat down to watch the TV my legs would be pulsating with anticipation and I could not concentrate on anything. I'd be there like a recumbent tap dancer, driving all to distraction.

A timid knock on the door heralded the first arrival. I skidded across the block floor linoleum, switching on the hall light as I went, only to see a single, aged female outline silhouetted on the porch. It was Mrs Davis, an ancient neighbour, in her tweed coat and headscarf.

Mrs Davis did not really hold with alcohol consumption on anything other than strictly medicinal grounds under the supervision of a doctor. Her objections were part religious, as she was a member of a strict Welsh Baptist chapel, and part general killjoy. She always spoke in a funereal whisper, whatever the subject matter, an earnestness that was both holier than thou and disconcerting. I supposed that had I truly believed, like her, that the end of the world was nigh and that we would shortly be judged for all our sins, I'd have kept a low profile as well. She always made me feel defensive and depressed.

She disappeared into the back room for a conversation with my mum and I made myself scarce.

"I'll wish you all good night and a happy New Year," she stated flatly as she emerged to leave, headscarf still in place and careworn face wrinkled in a permanent grimace.

She'd caught me at the foot of the stairs, trapped between her and the glass front door which was always cold to the touch. For an awful second, as she stood there, I thought she was expecting a kiss. I shuddered at the thought of her prune like skin and cold clamminess and, almost as if she sensed my discomfort, she turned to the door and departed. I felt both mean and relieved to see her leave.

Coming up the path, as she receded into the night, was none other than Uncle Robert, Auntie Mary's husband.

Uncle Robert was a short rotund figure with balding, Brylcreemed hair and a slight, short-person cockiness, always smiling and gesticulating. Five years before, I'd made a joke about Uncle Robert's old Austin car. It was neither funny nor amusing on reflection. I'd simply said that I hoped the engine didn't fall out.

Uncle Robert, told my dad, and anyone else who would listen, what I'd said, prefacing each telling with, "Can you believe what this lad said – sharp as a razor he is – he hoped the engine didn't fall out of the car – can you believe it?"

Funny it wasn't, but Uncle Robert always made me feel significant and appreciated with the retelling of that tale.

He'd always shape up like some past-it middleweight boxer when he first saw me, making to feint with a right jab and then catching me lightly with a left cross. "Got to keep your guard up son!" he'd chastise me.

If I'd anticipate his move and cuff him lightly back he'd be taken aback and declare to all, "Did you see that? Fists of lightning, this lad – never even saw it coming! Jack, get this lad a pair of boxing gloves and he'll make your fortune."

Uncle Robert was a professional barman by trade. He knew all the exotic drinks, gin and tonic, black and tan, snakebites and even rum and blacks. Why, you might wonder, was such a person not raking in the tips on this of all nights? Truth be told, there was always some tale of woe, some dispute, that meant that Uncle Robert never stayed at one pub or club for more that two years. On Boxing Day evening this year, there had been some dispute with his latest employer and he had walked out as a matter of principle. The way he told it, his parting shot had been, "and I've been thrown out of better places than this, you know!" But the look on Auntie Mary's face told a different story.

Anyway, the town's drinking establishments loss was my gain tonight, as, with a characteristic conspiratorial wink and gesture he beckoned me over to him.

"Got a job for you tonight if you're interested," he whispered, looking around to make sure he had not been overheard by any of the other adults.

"Yes!" I whispered loudly with probably too much enthusiasm.

"How do you fancy being my barman for the night?" Oh, to be esteemed by the professional! I nodded, hardly able to contain myself. "Mind you, it's a demanding job – I'm looking for a professional service and I'll make it worth your while for a job well done. Honest evening's pay for an honest evening's work."

We sidled through to the kitchen and he chose a half pint glass. Barman always chose a half pint glass he told me so that they could say they had "had a drink" with the person that tipped them but then pocket the money for the other half a pint. He showed me how to pour the bitter into the glass to get the perfect head. Not too slow otherwise you'd get 'witches tit', nor too fast or you might as well serve it in an ice cream cone. Fill it to the top and no half measures!

"Now then," he stated, "I need you to check on my glass every half an hour, without any word from me, refill it if it needs a freshener. If I need to go out to the kitchen to refill it myself then you're out of work. There's a tip for every drink you bring me."

And he jangled his trouser pockets which resounded with the sound of ample change.

"There's a bonus if you are around to fill my glass for midnight – you're on double time after then – only fair on New Year's Eve!"

I resolved to keep Uncle Robert in beer into the morning hours, and, although the money was a keen incentive, I'd have happily served him for nothing for all the efforts he made to make me feel important.

As the evening progressed, I did not falter in my duty to him and he was as good as his word, with a steady toll of sixpences discreetly pressed to my palm with a wink and a tap to the nose. At ten thirty he declared to my mum,

"This lad's a genius, is there nothing he can't turn his hand to? I see a great future for him."

I thought that if Uncle Robert was saying that, it must be true and it was very refreshing to be esteemed in this way, given the abuse I took on the estate on a daily basis.

The early quiet of the evening had now dissipated as guests had arrived like the tide. I'd managed to relieve the early comers of coats and had laid them down on my parents' bed upstairs, but in my absence, the arriving guests had overtaken me. I was left with a bewildering array of coats without owners to lug upstairs. I tried to guess whose was whose.

The sombre black woollen coat with the Pure Wool and Marks and Spencer labels in it was probably Uncle Ivor the vicar's. That would make the blue and cream check coat his girlfriend's. The family had not met this girlfriend before so there would be much tutting and cooing downstairs as she was appraised as a potential family member. It seemed particularly strange that I had an uncle for a vicar and that he was still in the business of going out with girlfriends.

Although all the family, especially my mother, treated him with a marked deference, he was not so different from the rest of us. I think he was as embarrassed as I was at the extra effort that went into the arrangement of one of his visits. He must have laboured under the illusion that we ate all our food off delicate paper doilies, which was definitely not the case.

I believed he simply had a bigger vocabulary than the rest of us and I could work the word 'eponymous' into a sentence with him without him batting an eyelid. I resolved to do this, and perhaps make mention of the, "silvern Wye at Tintern," which was not so far away from where Uncle Ivor had been away to study vicaring. I was sure his riposte would be, "the silvern Wye, so beloved of the romantic poets!"

Which would either make him really brainy, or with a lot more time on his hands in the daytime than is healthy for a working man. Either way I'd ask him who the hell the romantic poets were, as they had been tormenting me for some time. Well' perhaps not quite in those words, given his job.

The next coat was Uncle Jim's gabardine raincoat which smelt of buses and oil, the scents of honest labour. That would make the dark blue leather jacket which was butter soft to the touch and heady with peachy perfume, Auntie Linda's. I always thought she looked like the models from London who were occasionally glimpsed on the television and then receded to their party lifestyle in Chelsea or Carnaby Street, or wherever the fun and the action were more intense than in my hometown.

My younger aunts and older female cousins could always be distinguished from my mum's generation because they wore eye make-up. My mum would sometimes affectionately refer to the younger ones as, "flighty" or, "dolly birds" but she spoke more in envy than malice. I think she looked back to the heady days of the war when she was their age and younger and the excitement and danger that was available on a daily basis.

The late onrush of arrivals masked the fact that midnight was on us and I was beckoned with some urgency downstairs to join in the dinging of the chimes of Big Ben and the singing of Auld Lang Syne. I'd always had trouble with the whole concept of that song. "Should old acquaintance be forgot," – was it a statement or a question? By the second line, the raucousness had set in and the tempo had accelerated the words into meaningless gibberish. Except for Auntie Glad, who was still completing the first line, oblivious to the efforts of the throng.

Everyone had linked crossed hands and I had found myself, rather fortuitously, between Aunties Sarah and Linda, cocooned in a dash of perfume and eyeliner. Whether it was the headiness of the perfume, or the illicit beer and dandelion and burdock cocktail that I'd been imbibing all night I cannot say, but for the first time I'd found myself moistening my lips in anticipation of the kisses that would follow the finale of the song.

In that brief juncture between the end of the song and the drunken onset of a spontaneous and electric conga line, I suddenly felt part of a grown up world. I think Auntie Linda sensed it too as she kissed me full on the lips for what seemed like a passionate five minutes, but was in fact seconds. It was as welcome an invitation to the grown up world as I was ever likely to receive. Or perhaps it was just me imagining it, as Auntie Linda, to my disappointment, set off around the room kissing everyone else as passionately and perfectly.

From that night, when I was subsequently chosen by my family to be the tall, dark stranger to rush from the back door to the front carrying a piece of coal, I began to put down the things of childhood, not all at once, and not without some backtracking, but life was changing and I was changing with it.

EPILOGUE

The 1960s were drawing to a close. In the Reso, I had been under the impression that nothing had changed and nothing was ever going to change.

There had been some rumblings about The Beatles, the steam trains had given way to characterless diesels and the money was soon going to change, giving the people of my grandparents' generation the chance to go on about how they had all been swindled. But somehow, in my heart of hearts, I believed that things would always stay reassuringly the same. Same streets, same faces, same certainties.

How little I knew the forces that were at work behind the scenes. The series of events that overtook me next came as a surprise for which I was totally unprepared.

Kings Hart Books is a small, independent publisher based in Oxford.

Our other fiction titles:
The Invisible Worm by Eileen O'Conor ISBN 978-1-906154-00-4
The Reso by Ambrose Conway (educational) ISBN 978-1-906154-01-1
Meeting Coty by Ruth Estevez ISBN 978-1906154-03-5
Apartment C by Ruth Learner ISBN 978-1-906-154-06-6
The Price by Tony Macnabb ISBN 978-1-906-154-08-0
St Anthony's Fire by Rod Sproson ISBN 978-1-906-154-10-3

Coming soon
Beyond the Reso by Ambrose Conway
ISBN 978-1-906154-12-7

Also:
Nyabinghi by Shamarley Fontaine
The Jewel Keepers by Elaine Bousfield

Please visit our website at www.kingshart.co.uk for extracts and further information.

Available to order at bookshops or through online retailers.

Lightning Source UK Ltd.
Milton Keynes UK
01 December 2009

146994UK00001B/52/P